Girl Parts

Girl Parts

JOHN M. CUSICK

CANDLEWICK PRESS

First paperback edition 2012

The Library of Congress has cataloged the hardcover edition as follows:

Cusick, John.
Girl parts / John Cusick. — 1st ed.
p. cm.
Summary: The lives of David, wealthy and popular but
still lonely, and Charlie, a soulful outsider, intersect when
Rose, the female Companion bot David's parents buy to treat
his dissociative disorder, forms a bond with Charlie.
ISBN 978-0-7636-4930-2 (hardcover)
[1. Science fiction. 2. Interpersonal relations — Fiction.
3. Robots — Fiction. 4. Social classes — Fiction.
5. Dissociative disorders — Fiction. 6. Popularity — Fiction.
7. Family life — Massachusetts — Fiction.
8. Massachusetts — Fiction.] I. Title.
PZ7.C9644Gir 2010
[Fic] — dc22   2009047399

ISBN 978-0-7636-5644-7 (paperback)

11 12 13 14 15 16 BVG 10 9 8 7 6 5 4 3 2 1

Printed in Berryville, VA, U.S.A.

This book was typeset in Granjon.

Candlewick Press
99 Dover Street
Somerville, Massachusetts 02144

visit us at www.candlewick.com

For Wanda

and

for Sarah

O.

The room was empty and black save for the blue eye of the computer and the yellow wedge beneath the door. Shapes crouched in the darkness — the dresser, a desk, a bed with adjacent night table. The bed had a lived-in look, the tousled sheets littered with crumbs and stained with ink, cola, coffee. The stars-and-moons comforter lay bunched against the headboard, along with a threadbare teddy bear and Mary Poppins pillow missing its spangles. Books and magazines were shoved to the wall, into the gap, along with countless socks, balled underwear, lost pens, scraps of paper, and secret journals, their pages bulging with ticket stubs and pasted photographs.

It was quiet. The analog clock went *teck*.

As if on cue, the door opened, spotlighting the posters on the wall — Monroe, Dean, Bogart, and the tragic Entwistle. A girl in creased white pajamas shuffled in, arms full. She closed the door, shutting out the yellow glare, and set her burdens on the desk. She pressed the flat monitor button. The computer hummed. The blue eye watched.

She stood the blender, filled with ice, and the liter of Coke off to one side. She placed the third object, small and squat, before her like an offering.

"I'd like to thank you all," she said to the eye. "I can't tell you how much it means to me you came tonight."

The girl was slight, with a thin face, pale skin, and heavily lidded eyes. Her hair was limp, with electric red highlights, damp now and pulled back in a scrunchie. One strand lay against her cheek. Her fingernails, unpainted and chewed to the quick, were still soft and white from the shower.

She reached under the desk to plug in the blender, her pajama top riding up her back. In a tree outside, a small bird awoke and spied the sky-blue glow inside the room. It took flight, wings fluttering, and struck the window with a fatal crack, falling dead into the darkness. The girl sat up, oblivious, adjusted her top, and opened the squat bottle. She dumped two hundred crimson-colored pills into the blender and added the Coke. The blades churned, pureeing the mixture into sweet, slushy gunk. She dumped the concoction into a large drinking glass and took a sip. It tasted like a Coke slushie.

She clicked the mouse. A favorite old movie began. She watched and sipped, knees pulled to her chest. The star's name loomed on-screen in tall letters as the shades of a window overlooking a city street opened like lazy eyes. As those eyes opened, hers began to droop, and she felt suffused with a heavy warmth. One final swallow and she climbed into her beloved bed, pulling the comforter up to her chin.

. . . .

She was asleep before the opening titles ended, and by the time a dozing Jimmy Stewart appeared, her heart had stopped.

The blue eye stared. After ten minutes, it ceased recording. One by one, the 750 viewers logged off. The show was over. It had been her best-attended video blog to date.

The night Nora Vogel died, the power went out in Westtown, Massachusetts. Everything went dark from Route 290 south to Olive Lake. Televisions blinked and computers held their breath. The big map at the power station shut down. The grid had a disconnect, and dot by dot the colored bulbs representing the homes of Westtown popped off like Christmas lights.

David Sun lived in one of the big houses on the western shore of Horizon Lake. He was grounded for smoking. His mother had found his stash behind the hall hamper, so David was home alone, watching *Scarface* on Retro_Flix.com.

David's computer was a Sony Triptych, the kind with a three-monitor layout and content spiral technology. David's dad invented the Triptych, and his dad's company, Sun Enterprises, sold them. Each monitor scanned and responded to the others, so when David image-searched the new Cadillac Pinnacle on Monitor 1, Mon2 splashed the latest stats from Gearhead.com. Mon3 responded with a vid of Gearhead's top model, Cynthia Sundae, washing a Caddy in her bathing suit, and so Mon1 answered with condom ads. It went around and around, over and over again.

. . . .

Link by link the Triptych brought David from *Scarface* to Al Capone to James Cagney to James Dean and finally to StarryEyedStranger42.blogspot.com. Nora died on Monitor 2. The image was so clear, David could see her eyelids flutter.

He didn't know how to react (the monitors did: Mon1 flashed a webpage of Fast Meds for Low Prices). He decided to message his friends, to see if they'd seen it, to see what they thought. But just then the power cut, the yellow desk lamp dimmed and died, and David was alone in the dark.

Across the lake, Charlie Nuvola stood on the beach and stared at the yellow glare of David Sun's house on the opposite shore. Charlie cradled a suede jacket in his arms. The vintage leather smelled vaguely of soy sauce and the fruity perfume of a person he sincerely hoped he'd never see again. He didn't know about Nora Vogel's suicide. He didn't even own a computer. He just wanted to be alone.

And as he watched, the houses along the west bank went dark. A power outage. Charlie saw something prophetic in that. His house was off the grid. The generator continued to hum, and he identified with the lonely porch light burning away over his shoulder, self-sufficient.

Then there was a pop. The generator gasped, the porch light flicked off, and the yard went dark. He stood in the gloom until his eyes adjusted, and he could see the blue stars. They were winking.

. . . .

1. Charlie and David

Even before Nora and the power died, Charlie's and David's lives were mixed up together like pigments on a palette.

Charlie and David lived on two sides of the same lake, Horizon Lake, which wasn't a real lake but a man-made reservoir. Horizon Lake was three miles long and one mile wide and marked the center of Westtown. There were mansions along the west bank, trees along the east. The biggest mansion belonged to the Suns. It was a four-story glass palace, split down the middle like a dollhouse so that the family inside was always visible. At night the Sun house, true to its name, blotted out the stars, tossing its white shadow across the water.

The west-bankers had long ago bought the land on the east bank, so they'd have no ugly houses to mar their view.

The only lot they couldn't buy belonged to a botanist and his wife—Charlie's parents. The land had been in the family for years, and they refused to give it up at any price. The Nuvolas kept an old map of Westtown on their den wall. Charlie had once calculated that if he folded the map in half, Egg Lake in the south and Olive Lake in the north would lie one on top the other, and he liked the natural symmetry. If he folded the map the other way, Charlie's and David's houses would come together like button and clasp.

David and Charlie attended the same all-boys Catholic school on the other side of Route 290. Saint Sebastian's ran from sixth grade through twelfth. Charlie was one of the odd ones who transferred in freshman year, breaking up a homeroom that had been constant three years running. Saint Seb's lauded alternative teaching methods. Rather than moving from room to room throughout the day, students stayed at one desk, taking Web-based classes on personal computers, progressing at their own pace. It was all part of the headmaster's directive to "prepare young men for the modern virtual workplace."

The school was named for Saint Sebastian, who survived a thousand arrows. Sometimes Charlie could relate.

"Here comes Charlie Freak."

"Hey, it's Mr. Magoo! Hey, Magoo!"

"Gnarly Charlie. You get those glasses off an old lady or what?"

Charlie Nuvola was weird. He looked weird; he acted weird; he was interested in weird things. Worst of all, he didn't seem to know or care that everyone else thought he was weird.

Charlie was an early bloomer. The summer after eighth grade, his upper lip was dotted with stiff, greasy hairs, and by freshman year, he towered over his classmates. From his mother, Charlie inherited a frilly mass of dark hair that loomed like a storm cloud when he leaned in to describe — in his low, rumbling voice — a *fascinating* strain of artichoke just discovered in Guam.

At lunch, Charlie sat alone, reading the latest issue of *Botanica* or one of his dog-eared Danny Houston novels (a series from the sixties about a dashing boy who solves crimes from a helicopter). Boys at the nearest table competed to land the most French fries in Charlie's hair before he absently swept them away. David Sun was the reigning champion.

The only person who encouraged Charlie was Coach Brackage, who presided over the school's miserable basketball team. Charlie was recruited for one season, and though he was tall, his shots were wild and halfhearted. "Focus, boy!" Coach yelled. "Keep your eyes up! And don't run like you're wearing flippers, for God's sake!"

When basketball season ended, Charlie was glad to have his afternoons back. He liked to follow the brambled path behind the school, away from the bright parking lot where David Sun and his friends lolled half out of their cars, music booming through their walleyed speakers. The path lead into the woods. This was where Charlie fit. His big feet stepped easily between the rocks and knuckled tree roots, and the branches started just high enough for him to pass under without stooping. The clumsy bee making the lily dip, the lazy blink of a sunny patch when a cloud rolled across it, the distant mutter of dragonfly wings. Every branch, bug, and pebble was connected in a grand plan. This was Charlie's utopia — a world without people.

David Sun fit in by instinct. He had two best friends, John Pigeon (called Clay) and Artie Stubb. Clay, Artie, and David had sat together since sixth grade. Their row shifted from term to term, but the Pigeon-Stubb-Sun phalanx was never broken. The freshman-year arrival of Charlie Nuvola and another boy, Paul Lampwick, threatened to strand Clay in the back of the second row, but a last-minute transfer restored the natural order. Even so, the trio still resented Nuvola and Lampwick, who weren't lifers like them and who were both at Saint Seb's on pity scholarships. David, whose father's monitors topped every desk in the building, especially despised scholarship kids.

Girls liked David. He'd had a girlfriend — a beautiful blonde a year older than he, the star of every school play — until she dumped him on Labor Day. He'd cheated on her. It happened on Nantucket, which to David's mind was out of bounds and therefore fair game. It hadn't been satisfying. The girls on Nantucket were wild dancers, but tight as clams when he got them alone. Two were steamed open with weed he bought from the local hippie, but he still came home a virgin. They wouldn't even let him past third base. Later, he bragged to Clay and Artie, only to discover the base system varied from region to region, and in western Massachusetts, David had barely rounded second.

"Ah, don't sweat it, Little Dog," Clay said, putting an arm around David's shoulder. Clay, despite being overweight, somehow always had a girlfriend and liked to dispense advice. "See, you've got to make her want it. You've got to run your hand up and down her side, see, and then you kind of graze your thumb . . ."

"Jesus, Clay," Artie said, grinding out his cigarette. "You want to make me sick?"

"I'm trying to tell our boy how to get some boob. . . ."

"Some boob?" Artie held his hands as if cupping a bowl. "Boob is not a substance you can have *some* of. You can't quantify boob."

David laughed, but Clay just shook his head. "So what? You have *fewer* boobs?"

"Right," said Artie, laughing too. "You have *fewer* boobs, and *less* ass."

That killed all three of them, and they actually rolled on the sidewalk outside the Pavilion like a bunch of bums. It was a good night.

Then came the afternoon in September, two weeks before the power outage. Charlie biked home from school, leaned his rusty ten-speed next to his father's, and pulled open the whining screen door.

Charlie lived alone with his father, Thaddeus, who was a professor at Clark University on a sabbatical of undetermined duration. Thaddeus's passion was New England flora, and he spent hours in the backyard, pondering plants. Like Charlie, Thaddeus was tall. He had a long beard and bushy eyebrows that reminded people of the kitschy wax candles carved to look like tree-spirits. Absentminded by nature, he would crouch in a patch of poison ivy for hours with his field book, then come inside, muttering to himself, "Where did I put the Dr. Burt's?"

Charlie dropped his bag by the door. There were coffee dregs in the sink and pencil shavings on the table. Charlie deduced his father was home and had probably been doing the crossword. He put his hand to his chin (just like Danny Houston) and pondered what called him away.

The flushing toilet solved the mystery.

"Hey, pal, what's new?" Thaddeus said, emerging from the bathroom with the paper under his arm.

"Nothing."

Charlie downed his afternoon glass of milk in three swallows, then settled into the sofa. Drowsiness enveloped him like the musty cushions. No matter how alert he was at last bell, the comfort of home was like ether, usually knocking him out until suppertime. If the woods were his natural habitat, the Nuvola house, with its wood paneling and clutter of paperbacks and magazines, was his den. Nothing could touch him here, off the grid.

"This one's got me stumped," Thaddeus said, meaning the crossword. "What about a nine-letter word for *truest pal?* Begins with a *c?*"

Charlie mumbled a response. He couldn't do word games.

Through his thickening doze, Charlie sensed his father watching him. He opened his eyes. Thaddeus was in the La-Z-Boy, leaning forward, hands folded. Charlie had seen his father stare this way at unclassified blossoms. Charlie felt uneasy.

"So, I had my meeting with your school counselor today."

"Oh?"

"The test results came in."

The first day of school, Saint Seb's administered "personality adjustment profiles." Ten pages of questions like, "If you were a spoon, what sort of handle would you have?"

"The counselor, Dr. Lightly, she told me your results suggested maladjustment." Thaddeus rubbed his hands together, his voice casual, as if they were discussing the latest article in *Botanica*. "They think you're depressed."

"Wait, what? What do you mean?"

"She mentioned Fixol." Thaddeus scratched at the bare patch of skin under his right eye. Fixol was a popular antidepressant.

Depressed. The word closed like a lid on his brain. And the way his dad smuggled it home, into their den, and dropped it with no more than mild scientific curiosity. He felt sick. Thaddeus placed a hand on Charlie's knee. His pinky was smudged with newsprint and graphite.

"That . . . can't be right." Charlie swallowed. It felt like a walnut was caught in his throat.

"Do you feel depressed?"

"I . . . don't know."

Thaddeus exhaled, his mustache poofing outward. "Well, think about it. OK, pal?" He patted Charlie's knee and rose from the armchair.

Charlie's mother had always said, "Normal follows the path of least resistance." Charlie thought he chose—on some level—to be different, but what if he was wrong? Wasn't he happy? At least sometimes? In the woods? By himself? A test couldn't determine that, could it?

Suddenly he couldn't breathe. Darkness crowded him, filling his nose and ears. It was like drowning. He turned over and puked on the floor.

"Are you OK?" Thaddeus rushed to his side. Charlie's face was green. "Sorry, buddy. I should have thrown that milk out a week ago."

That night, Charlie tossed and turned until three. He went to his desk, turned on the light, and made a list of times during the day when he was happy. Then he made a list of the times he was sad. The columns were even but showed an obvious trend: Charlie was happy alone. He was miserable with others.

Then he rated, from one to ten, how he felt on average. He remembered when he was a kid, going swimming with his parents at Olive Lake, his dad hoisting him up on his shoulders, his mom laughing and taking a picture. That day was a ten.

He looked at the number he'd written. Three.

Charlie put his head in his hands and thought. He woke later, still at his desk, an oval puddle of drool on the blotter, his Afro dented on one side. He turned off the light and climbed into bed. He lay awake in the darkness for a few minutes, then whispered, *"OK."* In a moment he was asleep.

2. The Date

What Charlie found attractive in women were brains and personality—beauty optional, popularity an absolute no. On reconsidering, he decided he could stomach someone popular if he had to. His options were limited. Saint Seb's was separated from its sister school by a shallow ravine, a border Saint Mary's girls rarely crossed other than to the track behind the old gym—and track girls were tall, somber, and reportedly stuck-up.

Charlie decided on a theater girl. Twice a year the two schools staged a joint play, and by early September the cast was staying late for rehearsals in the Saint Seb's auditorium. Rebecca Lampwick was Mrs. Higgins in this year's production of *My Fair Lady*. She had big boobs, which she referred to as "the twins," and a laugh that started high and avalanched into her lower register. Charlie first saw her last year when, after basketball practice, he had crossed the auditorium to use the Coke machines. Then she'd been Mrs. Lovett in *Sweeney Todd,* and her big laugh and black eyes seemed to follow him from up onstage.

After two days of reconnaissance, he made his move. Rehearsal started at four, and from three fifteen to three thirty the cast lounged in folding chairs in front of the stage. Charlie entered through the fire door and crossed to the back. They were loud and carefree, ignoring him until he veered toward their loose circle. The chatter stopped. Charlie stood like a Sequoia in a thicket of elms. He cleared his throat. Rebecca, who'd been saying something to Eliza Doolittle in a goofy baritone, turned to the newcomer and smiled.

"What's up, buttercup?" (This in her normal tenor's register.)

"Hi." Three heavily edited flash cards were tucked reassuringly in Charlie's pocket. He focused and recited. "I was wondering if . . . you would like to come . . . with me on Friday night . . . to get some Chinese food."

"Iambic tetrameter?" Pickering asked. Higgins snickered.

That day Rebecca was wearing a billowy pirate's blouse and gypsy earrings, an outfit Charlie thought silly. But up close she was lovely, with skin as white and flawless as windblown snowbanks. The others waited in silent anticipation. They were an incestuous group and wary of outsiders, especially ones like Charlie, who in some circles was considered a jock, despite his dork status. Charlie swallowed and studied the scuff marks on the floor, only looking up when Rebecca spoke.

There was a lot Charlie didn't know about Rebecca. Her confidence was showy. She felt fat and repulsive because boys her age never talked to her. Only grown men seemed to like her. They shouted at her from their cars, which made her feel like a freak. Last year her history teacher grabbed her chest while driving her home from Model UN, a secret that constricted like a noose around her throat whenever she thought about it.

When Charlie stammered his invitation, that rope seemed to loosen enough for her to slip out. A normal date with a guy her age felt like a last-minute reprieve.

"Yeah. Yes. I'd really like that. Thanks."

The next week was endless. When final bell rang on Friday, Charlie was the first out of his seat. His preparations were timed to the minute with no room for dawdling. With no car and no permit, he arranged for a cab to arrive at six thirty. Their reservation was for seven. That gave him three and a half short hours to perfect his transformation.

The date required a complete personal overhaul, appearance-wise. Charlie planned to shed his fuzzy school self and expose the finer, hipper person he knew was underneath. "Show her your best self," said the men's magazine he'd purchased. For Rebecca he'd reveal the Charlie no one knew, the Charlie he'd been saving.

He imagined himself as a caterpillar morphing in the balmy cocoon of the shower stall. He scrubbed his skin raw and paid extra attention (optimistically) to the under-carriage. Charlie anointed himself with woody cologne and fruity moisturizer. He rarely shaved, and the process was like stripping paint. His new razor made several passes before each stippled red path was clear. He'd selected jeans, a white T, and his father's suede jacket with the fringed lapels — not because it was cool but because it *wasn't*. It was rebellious, quirky, and had an ironic intellectual charm — like him.

At 6:27 Charlie emerged, a leathery, woolly moth, smelling (due to the combination of cologne and moistur-izer) like roasted bananas.

The cab was twenty minutes late, and Charlie had to repeat the directions three times. At 7:03 they pulled into a lot across from Denny's. Rebecca lived in a drab apartment building on Cay Street, by the highway. Walking toward the door, Charlie spotted her sitting in the bright lobby read-ing a magazine. She was wearing a low-cut aquamarine cocktail dress of stiff, shimmering material like scales — a loud outfit, full of personality, which relaxed Charlie some-what. He called her name but she didn't look up. He called it again, thinking he really should have brought flowers, and walked into the invisible glass partition that bisected the lobby. The partition chimed like a gong, and Rebecca looked up to see Charlie clutching his nose and mouthing curses. She ran to the door at the far end, and when it opened, Charlie heard a radio grumbling.

"Oh, Jesus, I'm so sorry. Are you OK? They put this in last year because of break-ins. You know, for security. Let me take a look at your nose."

"I'm fine," Charlie said, his ears turning scarlet. "Really."

"They should put up a sign." Rebecca smiled. "You look really nice."

"You too. Should we go up to your apartment? Should I meet your parents now, or . . . ?"

Rebecca laughed a little socialite's laugh. "Oh, now's not a good time. It's just a mess up there and Dad's had a long day at work, so . . ."

"Oh. OK."

"Is that our carriage?"

"It is. I don't have my permit yet, so . . ."

"No, no. It's perfect."

She smiled again, and Charlie felt warm all over, even as his nose began to throb.

Dinner was at the Peony Pavilion, a pan-Asian restaurant with dancing after nine. The food was cheap and the carding policy lax, so it was a popular date spot. When they arrived, some public-school girls were smoking in the stone pavilion outside. Seeing them reminded Charlie of his men's magazine, *Nice!,* and its "Ten Surefire Dating Tips from Real Women." He could only remember one, contributed by Melinda, 21, of Brooklyn: "When leaving the bar, I always love it when he places his hand on the small of my back. It's sexy and reassuring. It sort of makes me feel owned — but in a good way!" This was Charlie's ace in the hole, and remembering it made him walk a little faster toward the golden entranceway.

A waitress in a flowered robe led them to a glass-topped table near the back. *Pavilion* and *Tax Included* were the only English words on the menu.

"I guess it's order by number, huh?" Rebecca said. "My luck, I'll wind up with boiled goat feet."

"I don't think they do those."

"Right."

"Do you like edamame?"

"What are those?"

"Salty bean pods."

Rebecca giggled. "Oh, Charlie, I like the way you talk."

Charlie took a sip of his water. He couldn't tell if she was laughing at him or not. What was funny about . . . ? Oh.

"Well, then you'll love number four," he said. Number four was Chicken Dong.

"Hm?"

"Number four. On the menu."

"Oh! Why?"

"Uh, because." Charlie coughed into his fist. "Because it's Chicken Dong."

"Dong?"

"Should go well with salty bean pods."

Rebecca blinked. "Oh. OK, now I get it. Ha, ha." She pronounced it as two words: Ha. Ha.

Charlie hid behind his menu. By the time the waitress brought the salty bean pods, he was ready to leave. Rebecca talked about her interests, which were theater and Romantic literature. "That's with a capital *R,*" she said. She preferred Shaw to Beckett, Lerner and Loewe to Rodgers and Hammerstein, and had no time for Stanislavski. She tossed these names out naturally, but to Charlie they were as foreign as the menu's squiggles. Gibberish. When it was his turn, he told her about the *Epigaea repens* he'd seen last week, rare this time of year.

"Is that a bird?"

"A flower."

She didn't know any of the scientists he mentioned — they weren't *that* obscure — and identified the posies on the waitress's sleeve as "lavender."

They spoke the same language, but their English was like Mandarin to Morse code. Their body language was no better. Rebecca sent signals Charlie didn't understand. When she leaned across the table to tease the fringe of his jacket, she was saying, "Charlie, aren't my breasts fantastic?" But Charlie heard, "Your clothes are intriguing; tell me more about them!" When she moved her shoulders to the music, she meant, "I love this song. Ask me to dance!" But Charlie thought she meant, "I'm so bored, I'm fidgety."

And at the end of the night, when she squeezed his hand and smiled sadly over the electric candle, meaning, "I'm sorry we didn't really hit it off," Charlie heard, "Now would be a good time to lean over and kiss me."

So Charlie went for it. Rebecca, who wasn't expecting a kiss at all, and certainly not before the check arrived, turned her head to look for the waitress and turned back in time to see Charlie's face making a poorly aimed dive toward her own. She yelped and jerked back, sending Charlie farther off course. He tried to abort but put his elbow in the soy sauce. He did kiss her — sloppily, on the chin — before falling almost into her lap, which had retreated with the rest of her a good seven inches from the table. To onlookers it appeared as if an Afroed cowboy had vaulted across the table at an unwilling date, when in reality he had leaned in gracefully (just at the wrong time) and his date wasn't unwilling (just very, very surprised). Charlie landed at her feet, and the two stared at each other in mute horror for three agonizing beats before the entire room erupted in applause.

Charlie sat back in his seat and they waited, not looking at each other, until the bill was at last paid. As they left, ignoring several cheers from the tables they passed, Charlie figured at least he had the small-of-the-back trick. But when he went to place his hand, the large bow on the back of Rebecca's dress was in the way, and since he couldn't put his palm on her butt, he pressed instead on her mid-back between her shoulder blades.

To Rebecca, who tended to take responsibility for everyone's misery, it felt like her date was bodily shoving her out the door. She felt she had humiliated Charlie. The look of startled hurt in his eyes when she yelped—actually yelped!—seared her. On top of that, she'd apparently made him feel bored and awkward during dinner. Now she took his stony silence for anger, and as soon as they reached the pavilion she dropped onto one of the cement benches and started to sob. Charlie wanted to give her space and so turned away, and misinterpreted Rebecca's sputtered explanations for inarticulate but furious blubbering.

They were alone until the cab came. Charlie opened the door for her. The cabby's radio played Johnny Cash, and when they pulled up to Rebecca's building, she muttered a hoarse "thank you" and disappeared, her skirt swishing behind her like a fish's tail.

As the cab's headlights swept the quiet lot, Rebecca appeared in her bedroom window. She fogged the glass with her breath and wrote what looked like seven digits of a phone number with her fingertip. The building receded, and Charlie tried to make out the numbers, and wondered why she would write them (he had her number already). Only the middle three were legible, 0-7-7, followed by maybe a backward five. As the cab pulled onto Cay Street, Charlie's tired brain groped one last time before he gave up and closed his eyes against the ghostly trees and the whole awful night.

■   ■   ■

Rebecca climbed under her down comforter and stared at the moon through her window. Her cell phone, which she'd left on her nightstand, chirped insistently. She silenced it— she would check her messages tomorrow.

Her head ached from crying, and her chest felt bound and tight, making it difficult to relax. As sleep began to crowd her thoughts, she thought back on the night and realized that *I'm sorry,* when read backward from the back-seat of a moving cab, fifty yards away, might not make sense.

3. Treatment

Like Charlie, David was an only child. His father was a textbook "busy dad." David couldn't picture him without his earpiece and laptop. That was fine with David. Mr. Sun worked hard to give his family nice stuff, like David's new Caddy, which was so black and smooth light seemed to slip right off it. What got to David was the way his father looked at him sometimes, like he was a bug in the system.

"What do you *do* all day, anyway?" Mr. Sun would bark after the second pre-dinner cocktail.

"I connect with the future," David would say, which was the Sun Enterprises slogan.

But he couldn't talk that way to his mother, who had feelings. She'd cried when she found his cigarettes, and cried again when he said they belonged to Lupe, the housecleaner.

"Oh, *Davie*. Why do you want to break my heart?"

Mrs. Sun was into spiritualism. Her twin had died a few years before, and she'd begun doing séances and buying crystals. She listened for a message from her sister, but so far nothing.

"Mom, you've got to be joking with this stuff," David would say.

"Oh, *Davie*. Why do you want to break my heart?"

It was the same conversation, over and over again.

One Wednesday morning, David was summoned to the counselor's office. The old school shrink had quit Monday. Probably they'd hired another old biddy like Dr. Lightly, who had legs like chicken wattles.

When he knocked on the door, a man's voice answered. The new doc was young, with tight tan skin and hair slicked back with oil.

"David," he said, standing to shake. He had a voice like cocoa butter. "I'm Dr. Roger."

"Is that a first name or last name?" David asked.

Dr. Roger chuckled.

Dr. Lightly had hung family pictures on the wall, but now Dr. Roger's diplomas loomed like an array of television sets. David read the names—Harvard Medical, the Child Study Association of America, and something called the Center for Young Adult Relations (signed by the director and founder, Dr. Froy). The goofy posters of cats and turtles were gone, too, leaving pale patches on the wall.

"So what's up, Doc?"

David sat in one of the squeaky leather chairs. Dr. Roger folded his hands. Dr. Lightly's rainbow-haired trolls had been replaced by a blotter, a telephone, and a little red wooden bird, the kind that dipped its nose over and over again into a glass of water. Dr. Roger touched its beak, and it started to bob.

"So, David. How are you feeling today?"

"Not bad."

"Good. I've asked your parents to join us."

David's chair squeaked. "Huh?"

"Hello, David," said the speakerphone on Dr. Roger's desk. "It's your father."

"Dad?"

"Hello? Is this working?" The voice on the phone was different now. Higher. David's mother. "I don't know if I'm doing this right. Hello?"

"I'm missing a lunch meeting for this, David," Mr. Sun's voice cut in. "It's that important."

The little lights flashed insistently. David glared at the doc. "What is this? An ambush?"

Dr. Roger put up both hands. "Whoa, there. Nobody's ambushing anybody, David. Your parents are concerned, and we all think an open dialogue is best at this juncture."

"Hello?" Mrs. Sun said. "David, baby, if you can hear me, this is your mother and we love you very much."

"Jesus, Evelyn," Mr. Sun said. "Fourteen years in that house and you still can't work the phones?"

"George? Is that you? I can hear you, but I can't hear David."

"I'm here, Mom," David said.

"Hello?"

Dr. Roger cleared his throat. "David, we'd like to talk to you about last Friday."

"What happened last Friday?"

"Perhaps you'd like to tell us?"

David did a quick inventory of all the rules he'd broken. Smoking, speeding, staying out past curfew . . . He shrugged.

"I don't know what you mean."

"Did you watch that girl kill herself?" Mr. Sun's voice crackled on the small speaker. "Did you?"

David hadn't thought about the suicide vid since Friday. He swallowed. "How did you know . . . ?"

"That's not really important," Dr. Roger said. "What's important—"

"I read about it on G-news and checked your browser history," Mr. Sun said.

"You went on my computer?"

"What did he say, George?" Mrs. Sun asked.

"*Your* computer?" Mr. Sun said. "Paid for it with your paper route, did you?"

"I think we're getting off point," Dr. Roger said, his smile tight. "David, what's important isn't that you watched it. It's natural to be curious about death. It's that you didn't intervene."

David started to defend himself but trailed off. Intervening had simply never occurred to him. He felt a vague shame, the way you would if you got to school and realized you'd forgotten to wear underwear. But that made you a spaz, not a bad person. And that seemed to be the implication, that he was bad.

"What was I supposed to do?"

"What about calling the police?" Dr. Roger offered. "Or her parents? You knew the girl, didn't you?"

"Well, I know she went to Saint M's . . ."

"So why didn't you *do* anything?" Mr. Sun crackled.

It *was* an ambush.

"Hey, people do weird shit . . ." David started. Dr. Roger scowled. "Stuff," he continued, "on the Internet. There's probably another sad chick mixing herself a death cocktail right now. *I* didn't make her depressed. *I* didn't force the pills down her throat. Why are you all acting like it's my fault?"

There was silence on the telephone. Dr. Roger folded his hands.

"David, how much time would you say you spend on the Web per day?"

"What does *that* matter?"

"Just estimate."

"Like, maybe six hours?"

"Is that counting school?"

"My classes are online," David said. "What? Am I in trouble for *that* now, too?"

David felt his skin grow hot. He loosed his tie.

"I keep telling you, David. You're not in trouble." Dr. Roger leaned forward, his features softening. "We ask because your parents and I feel you're too removed from real life. We're worried you didn't think to help that girl because you're disassociated."

"Disassociated?"

"Disconnected."

"I think we lost Evelyn. . . ." Mr. Sun said.

"I'm here, George, but I can only hear your half of the conversation."

"OK, so I didn't do anything," David said. "But neither did anybody else! If there's something wrong with me, there's something wrong with everybody."

"If everyone you knew jumped off a bridge, would you too?" Dr. Roger asked.

David had heard this before, and knew you were supposed to say no. But was that really true? If everyone jumped off a bridge, maybe there was a good reason. Maybe the bridge was on fire. If anything, the guy who didn't jump was the crazy one.

He crossed his arms and scowled. Mr. Sun went on about "responsibility" and Dr. Roger kept repeating "our modern age." Finally, Dr. Roger said, "David, if I were to recommend a treatment, would you be open to trying it out?"

"You mean like drugs?"

"No. More like a learning tool. It's very new, revolutionary in fact. It's designed to help young men like yourself learn to reconnect. It will help you forge strong human relationships."

"I already do that," David said. "I have mad friends." It was true. His Friends List was the longest at Saint Seb's.

"I'm talking about a more substantial, empathetic connection."

"So what is it?"

"Show him the catalog," Mr. Sun said.

Dr. Roger pulled a magazine from his desk. David flipped through the glossy pages. There was a photo of a guy and girl walking hand-in-hand into the sunset. There were graphs and charts and a schematic of intersecting lines.

And then it hit him.

"You're shitting me," David said.

"Does he love it?" Mrs. Sun asked. "Hello? Am I still on? Oh, damn it. I think I lost them."

Because instant messaging was forbidden in class, the boys passed notes. Charlie's desk was in the center, and a hub. Justin Hoek, who sat behind Derek Fini, was best friends with Sean Lafferty, who sat two seats ahead of Charlie. Justin never folded his notes, so Charlie knew what percentage of Justin's virginity was lost from week to week. Orson Orlick, who was, according to Justin's notes, "the biggest fag this side of Horizon Lake," passed notes of his own to

Paul Lampwick (Rebecca's little brother), though these were folded and Charlie didn't snoop. He'd given up trying to ignore the taps on his shoulder and now mutely passed communiqués without looking up.

When David Sun was pulled from class, the disruption inspired a barrage of notes, clogging the pipes, so that John Thomas's note went to Mark Curley and Mike Butkus's note wound up with Artie Stubb, who boldly flipped Mike the bird and said across the room, "Why don't you mind your business, fat ass?" The class's adult moderator looked up from his newspaper and gave Artie a week's detention.

Orson tapped Charlie on the shoulder. He'd neglected to fold, and Charlie read without thinking: *Hey, Lampwick. Do you think Nuvola banged your sister?*

Flames licked Charlie's collar. He tore the note to pieces. An idea seized him. He scribbled a proposition, signed Orson's initials, and passed it to Paul. The pale freckled skin of Paul's neck turned pink. He turned, glared at Orson, and hissed, "I *told* you that was a one-time thing. Now leave me alone about it, *fairy.*"

Tears stuck to Paul's blond lashes, and Charlie's snicker died in his throat. Both Paul and Orson went home early with stomach cramps.

That night, David spent three hours on Stadium, an interactive virtual games arena. He met Artie's avatar near the Doom Room. Artie was swinging a battle-ax at a family of terrified dwarves when David floated by.

AxHole1992 would like to chat with you, David's computer told him.

> **SunGod2.16:** hey dogg. wuz happening.
> **AxHole1992:** !!!did you see what I did to those dwarves!!!
> **SunGod2.16:** you messed up some dwarves man good job.
> **AxHole1992:** hells yes I did
> **AxHole1992:** wuzup?
> **SunGod2.16:** nthn much
> **AxHole1992:** why did u get pulled out of class? did someone in ur family die
> **SunGod2.16:** naw, nthn like that i basically got in trouble for that suicide vid
> **AxHole1992:** yeah that was some fckd sht.
> **SunGod2.16:** word
> **AxHole1992:** so r u grounded or ???
> **AxHole1992:** (p.s. wipe ur browser history next time, dude)
> **SunGod2.16:** I *DID* wipe it my dad is mad good with computers
> **AxHole1992:** lame
> **SunGod2.16:** yes
> **SunGod2.16:** so yeah i am basically grounded

David didn't want to tell Artie about the meeting. He wanted to talk about it, but couldn't let the guys know that his parents thought he was *disassociated*. He didn't want to end up like Nick Smalls.

Nick Smalls had been part of their crew freshman year. Clay knew him through football, and he was quiet and amiable. Then something happened over Christmas break — Nick was in the hospital for a few days. It came out that he'd been in a mental institution. He'd suffered an "episode" and now had to take medication. Happy pills. The pills made Nick different, sometimes mopey and sometimes loud and obnoxious, like he was drunk. His moods were totally unpredictable.

He'd been Clay's friend first, and it was Clay who'd always invited Nick to hang out. When Nick stopped showing up on Fridays, Clay said, "Yeah, I don't know. I guess he couldn't make it." But he said it so Artie and David knew Nick *could* make it but wasn't invited. David was relieved. It was hard being around a crazy. Also, it was creepy the way Nick just went nuts. It was like he'd been struck by lightning — at random. Nick was a conductor for misfortune, and standing too close was dangerous. So nobody was friends with Nick Smalls anymore.

AxHole1992: dude did I tell you I finally hit it with that viking chick?

Artie was talking about a bot they'd run into last weekend. Bots were simulated avatars created by Stadium's designers to make the site seem more popular. They were automated, without any real people controlling them.

> **SunGod2.16:** yeah man she was a computer sim, though
> **AxHole1992:** yeah but she had amazing tits
> **SunGod2.16:** that is the truth
> **AxHole1992:** so we hooked up
> **AxHole1992:** on the back of a DRAGON
> **SunGod2.16:** you are the pimp of this thing man
> **AxHole1992:** basically yes
> **AxHole1992:** hold on, let me show u the vid

David didn't feel like watching. He set his avatar to auto-respond and watched some television.

4. Rose

David waited at the zenith of the horseshoe driveway. He was freezing, even in his leather jacket. His gloves were just inside on the hall table. The car would arrive any minute, and until then he could stuff his hands in his pockets.

Except that he wanted to smoke. Smoking would calm him down.

David heard a buzz as the front gates opened and an unmarked van glided up the driveway, the trees and bushes reflected in its inky surface. The driver, a slim man with glasses and wispy white hair, got out.

"David Sun?"

"Yeah."

"Coleo Foridae. Sakora Solutions."

"Right." David's gaze drifted to the back of the van. "Is it in there?"

"Could I see some ID, please?"

David handed over his wallet. A side door opened, and two technicians in gray jumpsuits climbed out. Their uniforms had pink patches the shape of blossoms stitched to the shoulder. One of the techs opened the rear doors. Together they pulled a sleek, lozenge-shaped box onto the drive, tipping it upright so that it gleamed like a rocket. Or an egg. Emblazoned at eye level was a pink flower — the Sakora logo.

The driver handed David a digital signature pad. David signed, and the pad beeped.

"So what now?" he asked, eyeing the seamless case.

The techs climbed back in the van and the driver got behind the wheel. "Now she wakes up. Enjoy, son." The van rumbled back up the drive.

The Sakora logo protruded from the surface of the case like a button. David pressed it. Something hissed inside, and the panels of the box began to slide away. Steam rose from within, machinery turned and whirred, and the panels tipped outward so that now the egg was a padded pink flower blossom. The mist cleared, and she was standing there, eyes open.

This was how Rose was born.

When they were both five, Charlie and David asked their mothers where babies come from. Charlie's mom folded herself into an armchair, sat Charlie on her lap, and pointed to pictures in what Charlie had always thought was a book of sea creatures. She helped him sound out the scientific names.

David's mother had a more whimsical answer.

"When two people make love, a little blue fairy leaps from the daddy to the mummy, connecting them like a ribbon of light. And sometimes, the fairy leaves a baby in the mummy's tummy."

Would the fairies leave any more babies in his mummy's tummy? David wanted to know.

"No, Davie."

Why not?

"Because Daddy's fairies are lazy."

She was unbelievably, *unspeakably* hot.

David had taken Sakora's online personality test— favorite movie, most embarrassing memory, even really private stuff like "How many times a day do you masturbate (on average)?" But there'd been no "Do you prefer redheads?" or "Are you a tits man or an ass man?"

The Companion wasn't just beautiful; she was *his* kind of beautiful. Tumbling red hair, pouty mouth, emerald eyes, and that small, soft body he liked. With his crew, David hollered after spindly supermodel types. But privately he liked girls round in all the right places. And this girl was round in all the right places.

This *"girl."* There was a fiberglass skeleton under that creamy skin, and a CPU behind those eyes. But she stared back at him, eyes fixed to his, lips slightly parted, as if *he* was the miracle of science. David was speechless.

He stepped forward, swaying slightly. He never felt awkward in front of girls, but this was somehow different. *Say something!* David's mind, faced with unfamiliar territory, became a feedback loop, asking itself over and over again what to do. None of his trusty icebreakers seemed right, and so David resorted to a default, the lamest thing imaginable: a handshake.

Meanwhile, in Rose's brain, nothing was that complicated.

If David's mind was a loop, Rose's mind was an arrow. It pointed to David. The rest of reality, whatever didn't fall along the length of the arrow, was insignificant.

A satellite link connected Rose to a data bank at Sakora HQ in Japan. As her emerald eyes passed over the lawn, information queued for access. **Grass. Flower pot. Stairs. Driveway. Tree.** Each node was the center of its own web. **Tree** connecting to **Green, Poplar, Seasons, Paper** . . .

This complex veil, pierced by Rose's unwavering arrow, was a techno-semantic marvel. And yet at three minutes old, her thoughts were as simple as Dr. Roger's red wooden bird dipping its beak into a glass of water over and over and over.

David extended his hand. Without hesitation Rose shook it, and as she did, spoke a message:

"Hello, David. My name is Rose. It is a pleasure to meet you. We are now entering minute two of our friendship. According to my Intimacy Clock, a handshake is now appropriate."

"Oh! Uh, OK. I . . ."

"As we get to know each other, we'll have access to more intimate forms of expression." Here Rose cocked her hip and winked. "And I *am* looking forward to getting to know you better."

Inside Rose's brain, *mmonroe.exe registered *complete.*

David withdrew his hand. "Uh, right. Do you want to come inside?"

"I do."

"OK. Head on in, and I'll wheel your box around to the garage."

"OK," said Rose.

David watched her mount the stairs, admiring the view. She sure moved like a real girl.

David found her in the foyer. She had taken off her sweatshirt and tied it around her waist. At first she seemed to be admiring the marble columns, but no. She was just standing there, staring.

"Hey."

"Hello, David. It is nice to see you again."

"Yeah. Should you like, come up to my room, or . . . ?"

"Are you hungry? I could make you a sandwich. I'm very good at making sandwiches."

"Uh, sure," David said. "Kitchen's this way."

"Uh, great."

Near dusk, the Suns' kitchen lit up like a hall of mirrors. Sunlight bounded off the stainless-steel range and immense Sub-Zero, so that David had to squint. Rose was unperturbed. She set to work, going directly to the meat drawer. "So, what do you like? You have salami, ham, or . . . ?"

"Ham's fine."

Rose glanced over her shoulder. "OK, sit on down, and I'll serve you."

David sat at the counter, feeling like a little kid. Rose buzzed around the kitchen, pausing to ask where things were. She seemed less stiff already, more human, brushing a strand of hair from her face, licking a dab of mustard off her thumb. Even her speech was changing.

"So, tell me about yourself."

David rested his chin on his arms. "What's there to tell? I'm just a normal guy, I guess."

"What do you like to do?"

"I don't know. Watch movies. Hang out. Be awesome."

This last line was a joke, but Rose didn't laugh. She sliced his sandwich and slid the plate across the counter. *bettycrocker.exe registered *complete*.

"That's interesting." She folded her arms across the Formica and rested her chin.

David sat up. Rose did the same. He balanced his chin on his fist. Rose mimicked him.

He'd seen a video once of apes in the wild. The research-
ers acted like monkeys, crouching in the grass, scratching
their pits, hooting. After a while the apes relaxed and started
to play.

"You're like a researcher," David said.

Her smile didn't flicker. "I don't understand."

"Like a researcher that mimics apes to learn more
about them."

"I'm like a researcher that mimics apes to learn more
about them."

David laughed. "See? There you go."

Rose blinked.

In that instant, a query packaged in a photon launched
into space, ricocheted off a satellite, and penetrated the
Sakora data banks in Osaka. An answer vaulted back to
Rose's mind in the time it took her to blink.

**Simile: Comparing one thing to another to convey a richer
understanding.**

Rose had a richer understanding of David, how he
thought and how he spoke. And this made her glad. And her
gladness was . . . *bright like sunlight reflected off steel cabinets.*

"This is pretty good," David said, chewing.

"Thank you."

Rose prepared herself a sandwich. It was hard not to
stare at her, especially when she bent over to reach a low
shelf. At first he looked away whenever she caught him,

but eventually he just stared. She seemed to want him to. And she was *his,* after all.

"You're good with those hands. In the kitchen, anyway."

"Thank you."

David tried a more direct approach. "And the rest of you isn't too bad, either."

She glanced at him from under her bangs, her cheeks flushing.

"Oh. Well, I think you're . . . awesome."

David laughed again. He couldn't help it. This had to be the lamest flirting in the history of mankind. But he liked it. He liked her. She seemed . . . honest.

After, when Rose rinsed the dishes, David sidled up alongside her, wondering if her breathing quickened or if he imagined it. She smelled like strawberry perfume, and her skin gave off heat. Maybe this was all a joke. This was no robotic girlfriend. This was a beautiful chick hired by a company, a hot actress in a black tank top and tight jeans. David placed his hand on her shoulder and felt, for an instant, her warm softness. Then she electrocuted him with two hundred and fifty volts.

Blue light arched across the room. David heard a snap and felt a hot vise around his arm. His jaw clenched so hard it felt like his teeth might crack. The vise released, and he flew backward against the refrigerator door. An acrid smell hung in the air, and the room seemed hazy, either from smoke or his eyes crossing.

He stared at his hand. There was no blood, but the skin was an angry red. Rose was doubled over, clutching at her stomach, but her eyes were on him.

"Dude, what the hell!"

"I apologize!"

"Jesus Christ!" David shook his hand. "What the hell was that?"

"I am so sorry. My Intimacy Clock has a security system. Not telling you sooner was an error."

She stepped toward him, but he retreated around the counter.

"What are you, a freaking bank?"

"It's only temporary. There's a countdown. At two minutes you can shake my hand. After a little more time we can kiss."

She reached out to him, but David moved around her in a wide arc, heading for the sink. "Babe, if you think I'm putting my lips anywhere *near* you, you're crazy."

She lowered her arms and looked — if such a thing were possible — stung.

David ran his hand under the cold water. Rose stood away, her hands folded. "It is painful for me, too," she said quietly.

"What?"

"The shock. My pain receptors sense it, like yours. I enjoy your touch, but . . ." Her eyes shone with — *tears?* "It's not allowed."

"Who doesn't allow you?" David's arm muscles were beginning to unclench.

Rose blinked, twin teardrops sliding down her cheeks. "I have failed to be pleasing."

"All right, all right. You can turn off the waterworks."

"I can't. They're involuntary."

At those words, something in him melted. He sighed and smiled weakly. "And that was just a shoulder. Imagine if I grabbed your boob."

Rose smiled through her tears. "You're being funny."

"So you *do* have a sense of humor," he said. "Are you OK?"

She nodded. "I'm experiencing embarrassment."

"Me too."

She wiped a tear.

"Do you want to go watch a movie?"

"Yes."

"Can I take your hand?"

"Yes."

David laced his burning fingers between hers and squeezed.

Rose's egg contained a large black case — her luggage. Inside, David found a certificate of ownership (he'd have to get a frame), a pair of jeans, green sneakers, black pumps, sweatpants, three designer T-shirts, a tweed skirt, tights, a black cocktail dress (he couldn't wait to see her in *that*), checked boxers and a long cotton T for sleeping (that, too), cherry-blossom socks, a Dopp kit with twenty gel packs labeled "ablutions," jewelry, makeup, and a black plastic bag of "unmentionables."

There was also a disc, which Mr. Sun played on the den entertainment system. The family gathered around, the parents in the armchairs, David and Rose on the loveseat. The Sakora logo appeared on screen. Music swelled.

"Welcome to Sakora," a woman's voice said. "Solutions for Life."

The screen darkened and faded in on an empty classroom. A woman with graying chestnut hair and a pencil skirt leaned against the teacher's desk and smiled.

"Hello, and welcome to Sakora Solutions' Companion Program Welcome Presentation. I'm Dr. Paula Love, chief behavioral specialist here at Sakora Solutions, and your guide through this instructional tutorial. Over the next sixty minutes . . ."

"Do we have to watch the whole thing?" David said.

Mrs. Sun shushed him.

Dr. Love gestured to the chalkboard, where three words were written. "Did you know that more than forty percent of young adults experience chronic feelings of disassociation . . . discomfort . . . and depression?"

"No, I didn't know that," David mumbled.

"In our digital age, interpersonal relationships are increasingly crowded out by electronic distractions."

A boy David's age ran in front of a green screen, pretending to duck the images of computer monitors, cell phones, and game systems dive-bombing his head.

"I feel so disassociated!" the boy shouted. "Disassooooociated!"

The music switched from menacing to hopeful. Dr. Love, now in a relaxed sundress, strolled through a sunny park.

"Studies have shown that young men from thirteen to seventeen are particularly at risk. Cases of anhedonia, moral apathy, and even suicide are on the rise. That's why there's Sakora Solutions' Companion Program."

Over Dr. Love's shoulder, a boy and girl walked hand in hand.

"Using the mechanics of punishment and reward, the Companion dissuades dehumanizing behaviors and encourages healthy human interaction." The boy, leering, palmed the girl's ass. A spark (added in postproduction) snapped at his hand. The boy withdrew, pouting.

"That's not how I remember it," David said under his breath.

Dr. Love continued. "The Companion's Intimacy Clock measures the degree of interpersonal connection over time . . ."

Mr. Sun checked his watch. "Maybe we can skip a bit." He hit the advance button. Dr. Love (pantsuit) strolled through the halls of an enormous library.

"Ugh, that outfit," Mrs. Sun said.

"Your Companion has access to nearly a million logographic and encyclopedic entries, including a vast database of nonverbal facial and body-language cues. But she still has a lot to learn!" Dr. Love chuckled stiffly. "Because our world is always changing, Companions are not programmed with slang, jargon, or technical language. But thanks to Sakora's ABC Protocol, she will quickly absorb new words and phrases and incorporate them into her vocabulary."

"Like *groovy* and *far out?*" David said.

Rose blinked. "Far out?"

"Don't actually say that," David said.

A man in a white lab coat joined the doctor. The caption read *Dr. Samuel Froy, Chief Developmental Engineer.*

"Well, hi there, Sam. Why don't you tell the folks at home a little bit about how the Companion's brain works?"

"Thank you, Paula." Dr. Froy had a thick foreign accent, so it sounded like, "Zank you, Paula."

"Ze Companion's mind is comprised of two parts — an emotional core, where her desire for you is located, and a strict moral code, which checks this desire. Like our informational database, this moral code is connected via satellite link . . ."

"They lose me with this technical stuff," Mrs. Sun said, reading the back of the DVD case. "Is there a special features section?"

"Hold on, he's saying something important," Mr. Sun said.

"This is a delicate balance," Dr. Froy was saying, "between impulse and control. This is why your Companion must never enter a lead-lined room or be submerged entirely in water. Doing so severs the link, and will cause the unit to be . . . *decommissioned.*"

To illustrate, the image returned to the girl in the park, who, in a surprisingly realistic animation, exploded in a fiery ball.

"Oh my," said Mrs. Sun.

Rose blinked.

When the DVD was over, Mr. and Mrs. Sun retired to the dining room to eat the meal Lupe had prepared. David was in the kitchen, microwaving a pizza. Rose was alone in the hall. Eating pizza with David meant first processing her lunch, and this required privacy. Her body had reduced the food to vapors that needed expelling. Rose burped.

She could see Mr. and Mrs. Sun through the glass doors separating the dining room from the foyer, candlelight gleaming on their twin wine glasses.

In the den, David watched television while tipping a slice of pizza toward his mouth.

"Do your parents like me?" Rose asked.

"I don't know."

"Do you want them to?"

"I don't really care."

"I don't either."

She settled back, careful not to touch David's shoulder. On-screen, a helicopter exploded.

"You know, you don't have to do everything I do."

"What do you mean?"

"I mean, you don't have to just think what I think."

"Don't you want me to agree with you?"

"Well, yeah but . . ." He scowled, thinking. "Look, you want me to like you, right?"

Rose bounced on her cushion. "Oh, yes! More than anything."

"OK. Then I'd like you to act normal. And normal people think their own thoughts. They don't always just agree with each other."

Rose nodded. "How often would you like me to disagree?"

David let out a long, slow breath. "OK, think of it like this." He scooped a handful of jelly beans from the bowl on the table. Some were sour, and some were sweet. "Try one of each."

Rose popped one, then the other into her mouth.

"Now. Which tastes better?"

"I don't know."

"Well, I like the sweet ones better."

"Sweeter is better."

"Are you just saying that because I said it?"

"Yes."

David sighed.

"Well, I just decided I like the sour better. So now we disagree."

"All right," said Rose. "Sour is better."

David pulled at his hair. "Jesus!"

"I'm sorry! I'll try again." She selected a sour jelly bean. It was unpleasant. Disagreement was unpleasant. David liked disagreement. So . . . "I've decided I do like sour better."

"Really?"

"Yes."

David grinned. "Awesome. See? You prefer sour, and I prefer sweet. It's a difference of opinion."

"And that's what you want?"

"Yes."

"Good."

She offered the bowl to David. He took a handful and dropped them into his mouth. "I like you."

"I like you, too." She adjusted herself so their shoulders were touching. "You can put your arm around me now, if you want."

"Are you sure?"

"I'm sure."

He draped an arm around her shoulder, and Rose settled into the crook of his body, the bowl balanced expertly on her knee.

5. Friday

The next morning David met Artie in the parking lot.

"What are you so smiley about?" Artie asked.

David locked the handlebars of his motorbike and lowered the kickstand. "I don't know. Just in a good mood, I guess."

David was in a very good mood. Thoughts of Rose danced in his head. It wasn't like dating a new girl (he couldn't show her off), and it wasn't like getting a new bike or car (he couldn't bring her to school). It was something new, something private, and he liked it.

David wondered what Rose was doing. She was probably in the guest room his mom had set up for her. Rose "recharged" for six hours a night. But what about during the school day? Maybe she'd read magazines or surf the Web.

Or maybe she'd just stare at the wall, like a laptop on *hibernate*. When he left, she'd said, "I'll miss you, that's all."

Boys in pigeon-gray jackets flocked toward the front doors, past the abstract statute of Saint Sebastian on the lawn—a ten-foot-tall lead pipe intersected by a hundred metal rods. Someone had tied a red-tipped necktie to the top, and it snapped in the wind.

"You coming tonight?" Artie asked.

"Yeah, I'll be by later."

Artie glanced over his shoulder. He had a way of looking guilty even when he'd done nothing wrong. "Whose turn to bring beer?"

"Clay's," David said, stuffing a pack of minidrives into his pocket.

"We have an assembly today about the suicide vid thing," Artie said. "I'm all paranoid since your dad called you out. I wiped my browser history like ten times after that."

The smile dropped from David's face. "Yeah, well. Let's not talk about that, OK?"

"Why're you all weird about it?"

David slammed his locker and spun the lock. "I'm not weird. I just don't want to talk about it."

Artie shrugged.

At noon the auditorium doors opened and grades nine through twelve of Saint Mary's filed in. The girls sat in alphabetical order on the left side — standard practice for coassemblies. The boys' side was empty, inspiring general disappointment. Onstage the faculty sat in folding chairs, hands folded. Mr. Branch, the janitor, struggled with a tangle in the stage rigging. He glanced into the rafters and jostled the line to no avail. Seeing that the girls were seated, he shrugged and shuffled off.

Headmistress Droit, fresh eyeliner beneath her red eyes, tapped the podium microphone. Feedback squealed. The girls covered their ears.

"Ladies, quiet, please. In the back, Ms. Pigeon. Eyes open. There is no napping during assemblies." She cleared her throat and glanced at her notes. "As you all know, last week a great tragedy befell our school. You read the details in the letter sent to your homes on Monday. In a moment, the boys will arrive and our new student counselor, Mr. Rogers . . . excuse me, *Dr.* Rogers . . . will speak. But first, I want to address you, Nora's classmates, about this terrible event."

She switched index cards.

"I was approached by a number of girls about a memorial." The girls looked at each other, wondering who. "In that spirit, our art teacher, Mrs. S., has thoughtfully arranged a moving tribute. Please look under your seats."

Each girl found a small envelope. Inside was a note in elegant script and a heavy metal pin, painted to look like a red robin.

"'To show our solidarity with the Vogel family,'" the headmistress read aloud, "'we ask that you wear these brooches in memory of our dear Nora. These little birds shall not fly away but shall remain forever pinned'"— she frowned at the card, then flipped it over—"'to our hearts.'"

There was weak applause. A girl in the front row stuck the brooch to her blouse, sagging the material and exposing her bra strap. She rolled her eyes, unclasped the pin, dropped it into her purse, and zipped the bag shut.

"And now," the headmistress continued, putting away her notes, "I would like to invite you to share your memories. . . ."

Just then the rear doors burst open, revealing Mr. Gauche, headmaster of Saint Seb's, followed by four hundred shoving, chattering, gray-jacketed boys in loose formation. The headmaster was shouting, "Gentlemen, quiet. Quiet, damn it! So help me, I'll put you through that wall, Stubbs. Luther! Is that gum?"

The girls twisted around, straining to spot their favorites. The boys, sifting into alphabetical order, flocked to their seats across the aisle, almost, but not quite, close enough to touch. This was the pattern of every coassembly for as long as they'd been in high school: David Sun sat across from Vonis Summer, who was thrilled to sit so close to the hottest sophomore; a few rows back, Charlie was similarly paired with obese Cynthia Nuun; and in the last row, Wallace

Watts leered at the shiny legs of his cousin Willow, who did her best to ignore him.

Somewhere in the middle Charlie spotted Paul Lampwick's pinched shoulders. He glanced at the corresponding section of girls and jumped to see a pair of black irises staring back. The heavy lashes blinked twice before Rebecca looked away, her ponytail swinging. Charlie stared at his feet.

Gauche took over the podium. In the chaos, Mr. Branch tried again with the rigging, and both men stared anxiously up. Finally Gauche waved him off. "Now," boomed the headmaster, who never used a microphone, "this is a difficult, sad time. I'm sure you're all feeling a mix of unusual emotions. Confusion, anger, uncertainty, rage, or even . . . unsureness." Unlike Droit, Gauche winged speeches. "You may want someone to talk to. Unfortunately, our former counselor, Dr. Lightly, has retired."

"Probably feels guilty," someone hissed.

"But to replace her, we have a gentleman who has counseled students across New England, most recently at Saint John's in Shrewsbury, and also in the Worcester public school system. When he heard of our tragic loss, he offered to abandon his freelance work and take a position as our full-time student counselor. He is a pioneering researcher of Teen Disassociative Disorder, which likely played a role in the tragic passing of Ms. Vogel, who, I understand, was a . . . uh, tragic actress. Dr. Roger?"

Dr. Roger rose, shook Gauche's hand, and took the podium. He smiled sadly, looking out over the crowd.

"My name is Dr. Roger. Some of you have met with me already, and I hope to meet with each of you in time. For now, though, one question: how *are* you today?"

Silence.

"No, I mean it: how are you today?"

The students looked left and right uncertainly.

"Tell me. How are you?

Twelve hundred voices said, "Fine."

"That's the easy answer," said Dr. Roger. "But I want you to reach for the hard answer, which is how you really feel, down inside."

After that, no one paid attention. Cell phones were smuggled out for texting, notes were passed, come-ons mouthed. Couples with aisle seats (there were four) ached to reach across and brush fingers. The less datable slipped in earbuds or stared at their hands. Charlie felt something strike his shoulder and looked back to see Artie Stubb holding a rubber band and grinning. Charlie retrieved the flung paper clip and fiddled with it.

When the students were dismissed, everyone rushed to the center aisle, chatting, laughing, making plans. A freshman squealed and batted a hand away from her backside. Charlie was in no rush to return to class and lingered. He saw Rebecca make her way out, flanked by two juniors. They were intercepted by Mr. Throat, the history teacher, who put a fatherly hand on Rebecca's shoulder. She laughed, shrugged, and ducked away, suddenly reversing directions and heading for the back door.

Her eyes met Charlie's. Her grin had vanished, and for some reason she looked flushed and uncomfortable. He opened his mouth to say he wasn't sure what, but she hurried toward the stage, where Mr. Branch had finally loosened the rigging. She glanced once back at Charlie, her face burning scarlet, and exited to the parking lot.

The closing door echoed in the now-empty room. Charlie was alone, clutching the paper clip. He threw it. The clip went wild, bouncing off the podium. As if in reply, something popped, a length of rope went hurtling up into the rafters, and with a zipping sound the five-by-ten banner of Nora Vogel's class photo fell to the ground with a metallic crash.

At 1:45 Paul Lampwick returned with red-rimmed eyes from his one-on-one with Dr. Roger. Charlie lumbered slowly to the guidance office, trailing his fingers along the lockers.

"Charlie, come in."

Dr. Roger stood to shake hands. His palm was soft and oily. He smelled like aloe.

"Thanks for coming down." His tone was cheery, almost relieved. The doc shook his head. "I've seen so many kids today, it's making my head spin. I feel like I should just set up a little tape recorder that says, 'Yes, it's perfectly normal' over and over again." He grinned.

Charlie relaxed a little, settling into his chair.

"So, what's up?" Dr. Roger asked.

"Nothing."

"Nothing? Everything fine?"

"Completely fine."

Dr. Roger raised his eyebrows. "Good! I'm glad to hear it." He flipped through Charlie's file. "Your classmates had some nice things to say about you."

Charlie blinked. "Um, I'm Charlie Nuvola."

"Sorry?"

"I think you're confused. My name." Charlie pointed to the file. "It's Charlie Nuvola."

Dr. Roger glanced down, then back at Charlie. "Is it so surprising your classmates spoke fondly of you?"

He shrugged.

"Would you be less surprised if they were nasty?" Dr. Roger waited a beat. "Or if they said nothing at all?"

Charlie folded his arms. Again that feeling of a lid closing on his brain.

"That's all right, Charlie. The most independent thinkers are often the quietest. Thing is, we keep things to ourselves when we don't think anyone will understand." Dr. Roger waited a beat. "Do you ever feel that way?"

"Doesn't everybody?"

"I have in my notes that Dr. Lightly prescribed Fixol, an antidepressant."

"She recommended it. She didn't prescribe it."

Dr. Roger tapped his lips with an index finger. "Well, if you don't think you need it, I agree."

Charlie was shocked. "Really?"

"I don't believe every problem can be solved through drugs, Charlie. I like to look at human behavior and interactions."

Charlie sat back in his chair, letting out a long breath. "Good."

Dr. Roger flipped over a page. "It says here your mother left a few years ago."

"That's true."

"Would you like to talk about it?"

"Not really."

"Mother gone. Not many friends. Close with your dad?"

Charlie's eyes flicked to the carpet. "Yes."

"Until recently?"

Charlie's breath caught. He met the doctor's eyes.

"These are difficult years. The parent-child relationship becomes strained, especially in a single-parent home."

Charlie shook his head. "Well, that's not us. We're friends."

Dr. Roger nodded slowly. "Good. Good." He took a sip from the tumbler of water on his desk. "And friends are always there for each other. Look out for one another. I bet you look out for him sometimes, too."

"Sometimes. What's wrong with that?"

"Nothing. I'm sure it's made you very independent, which is good. Means you're mature. Of course, it also means you've got to rely on yourself a lot. Be your own parent. Decide for yourself what's good or bad, right or wrong. I'll bet you make lists. In a journal, perhaps? Or maybe just in your head when you're by yourself. Lists of rules. Principles. Things to rely on, that you decide for yourself."

Charlie thought of his happiness list, but said nothing. Dr. Roger went on.

"Most people haven't had to be self-reliant, so they aren't smart enough, or strong enough. Which makes them selfish and reckless. And sometimes it feels like . . . it's best to just avoid people, and their flimsy rules. Being alone becomes its own rule, doesn't it?"

Charlie's throat felt tight. He tried to swallow but couldn't.

"But being alone is hard. It's lonely, and it's sad. Maybe now and then you meet somebody who's different. Different like you. But you *have* to be alone. Because if you don't *have* to, then maybe you're lonely for no good reason. Maybe it's not by choice." Dr. Roger leaned forward and looked Charlie in the eye. "Charlie, I'm here to tell you that you don't have to be alone. No one should ever be alone. That's a rule *I* have." He folded his hands. "Do you think you can borrow one of my rules?"

Charlie blinked. He felt coolness on his cheeks. He touched them, and his fingertips came away wet. He stared at the tears, shocked.

"Charlie, I don't think you're depressed." He closed Charlie's file and pushed it aside. "It makes sense you feel . . . disconnected. You've become disassociated from the world, because at large, it has failed you." Dr. Roger leaned back, steepling his fingers. "If I were to recommend a treatment, would you be open to trying it out?"

David couldn't stop thinking about Rose all day. He decided to cut last-period gym and go home early. He sneaked out the back door and jogged toward the parking lot. A row of cars was parked on the grass by the auditorium, one a white Ford Taurus with the license plate WATTS1. A woman in a reindeer sweater was haranguing a pair of exhausted stage-hands. It was Mrs. Hynes, Saint Mary's theater director.

"Well, we can't do the Ascot scene without Mrs. Higgins! Why would she just take off? She knows we have rehearsal today."

David decided to cut across the field, but she'd already spotted him. She waved in his direction, her scowl melting into a syrupy grin, purple heels sinking into the mud as she hobbled over.

"David! Oh, I'm so glad I caught you. Listen, swim season doesn't start for another few weeks. What do you say you audition for *My Fair Lady*?"

David adjusted his bag and stared longingly at his bike, just a few yards away. Mrs. Hynes spooked him. She was nice enough, but desperate-seeming. Last year he'd seen her boobs when she bent to recover a dropped coffee mug, and he sometimes wondered if it was an accident. The experience scarred him.

"Aren't auditions over?"

"David, honey, it's been a disaster. My Mrs. Higgins is MIA. The whole cast is so maudlin since that girl died. You know she auditioned, don't you? She didn't have star quality, and that's what I told her. Disturbed person, clearly, poor little thing. And that dyed hair, yuck. Anyway, Orson dropped out, which is a tragedy because he's the best dancer in the school, and I remember you auditioned for the part of Anthony last year, and you had a very passable singing voice, so what do you say, huh? You'll do it?" She batted her false eyelashes.

"I'd like to, Mrs. Hynes, but I've got a lot of schoolwork."

She looked at him sideways and smiled. "I think you're running off to see a girl."

"I'm just really busy."

"I know what you're up to. Oh, to be young again. Of course, it wasn't *so* long ago that I was your age. . . ." She put a hand on his shoulder, and something in David's stomach lurched.

"Well, I've got to go."

"You'll come to the play, won't you?" Her hand slid down to clutch his fingers.

"Sure thing," he said, breaking away. He made for his bike at a dead run.

■   ■   ■

Rose was on the den computer.

"Hey, what are you up to?"

She turned at the sound of his voice and grinned. "Hello." She stood and wrapped her arms around his midsection.

"We've graduated to hugs, huh?"

"Friendly hugs, yes," she said, pressing against him.

Friendly for you, David thought.

"Look what I learned how to do today." She'd folded a piece of his father's stationery into the shape of a bird. "If you fold one part close to another part in just the right way, it makes a shape of something else. Isn't that interesting?"

"You learned origami?"

"I can only do the bird so far," she said. "Do you want me to show you how?"

"Later," David said. "Come on. Let's watch some TV."

That evening, David rapped on the French doors and waved to his parents, who were eating dinner. Mr. Sun pointed at his watch, meaning, "Back by curfew," and Mrs. Sun smiled with sad eyes, meaning, "If you smoke tonight, my heart will break."

"Let's take a ride," David said.

The garage lights were bright as a near-death experience. The 'Vette and the Maserati slumbered side by side. David's motorbike was next, sharing a stall with Rose's egg. At the end was his Cadillac Nightbird.

David loved to drive. It tantalized him. The pressure

pushing him into his seat was like a barrier he dared himself to break through. He drove faster, pushed harder, wanting to find out what was on the other side.

Soon they were out on the dark road. David took the first bend at sixty.

"Isn't this fun?" David said, pushing the pedal toward the floor.

"Yes," Rose said tentatively.

The dark trees flicked by, becoming indistinguishable from one another. David knew these roads by muscle memory and made the slightest adjustments, coaxing the car, soothing it, giving it what it wanted. He wondered if this was what sex was like.

David felt something brush his knee. Taking his eyes off the road at this speed was insane, but he glanced down long enough to see Rose's hand clasp his knee. Hot panic coursed through his body. Shock him now and they'd be wrapped around a tree before he could say "ouch." But there was no shock, just the pressure of her hand and the whisper of her breath.

Finally, David slowed and pulled onto a rocky side road. David grinned. "Was it good for you, too?"

Rose was flush, her breathing labored in an excellent simulation of human terror. Her hand remained clamped to David's knee.

"We could have crashed."

"Not likely," David said. "I'm pretty in control of this thing."

"We *could* have crashed," Rose said, lingering on the new word. *Could*. "We could have stopped functioning." Die, her mind embellished. Deactivate. Decommission.

"Yeah. I guess. That's part of the excitement, though."

David brought the car to a stop and killed the engine. "Come on. We walk from here." They climbed out of the car. "You're shaking," he said.

"It's just excess adrenaline. It will dilute momentarily."

"Well, come on." He took off into the woods. Rose followed. The lake's black smear was visible through the trees. Her brain assembled another simile, folding its edges together. She trembled . . . *like water rippling*.

6. The Campsite

On Friday nights, David, Clay, and Artie met at the campsite. It was a few miles northeast of the lake, no houses around. To David, it was evidence against Dr. Roger's and his parents' diagnosis.

"They think I'm all zombied out by computers and the net."

"Zombied?" Rose asked.

"Brain-dead. But me and the guys chill here and get back to nature. We connect out here, you know? But not in a queer way."

"Queer?" David's usage conflicted with the definition she had.

"Gay."

Deeper into the woods, lights flickered and voices bounded through the trees.

"The point is, I'm not disassociated. Though I don't mind having you around." He stopped and turned to her. "They can think I'm crazy if it means I get something as sweet as you."

Rose's blush was invisible in the gloom. David leaned in, but she ducked away, nearly stumbling over a tree root.

"I'm sorry," she said. "Not yet."

"Shit." David kicked the ground, and grit and pebbles sprayed her ankles. "All right. I guess I've had to wait before."

"Before?"

David resumed walking, and Rose hurried to catch up. "Oh, and listen. The guys don't know you're a Companion, and I'd like to keep it that way. They'd think I was nuts. Or so lame, my parents bought me a sex doll. So just pretend you're from out of town, OK?"

"Ii yo."

David stopped again. "Wait. What's that?"

"Nihongo wo hanashitara dou darou?"

"Are you speaking Japanese?"

Rose nodded.

David laughed. "Not *that* out of town. American."

"OK."

"Great," David grumbled, making for the campsite. "I'm sure this will work."

. . .

Farther on, they came upon another car parked in the weeds. It was black like David's, but less shiny. A girl was in the passenger seat, her head flopped to one side, eyes closed.

"Clay's sister," said David. "It's her car. Clay doesn't have his license yet."

"Is she recharging?"

"She's passed out." He shook his head. "Come on, it's just down here."

The campsite was an abandoned house foundation. Cement stairs descended to an overgrown pit with chunks of rock and slabs of iron. In the center a fire threw crazy shadows on the walls. Three people sat on the iron I beams—Clay, Artie, and a figure in a hooded sweatshirt.

"The Sun God arrives," Clay thundered, getting to his feet. "How kind of you to grace us with your presence."

Clay punched David in the shoulder and jumped back into a boxer's stance. He was quick for a big guy.

"Come on, Sun. Let's go. You and me. I'll pummel that swimmer's ass."

"Get out. You'd have a coronary before the first bell."

Clay laughed and handed David a beer. Artie nodded hello.

"Who's the redhead?"

David put his arm around Rose's shoulder. "Boys, I'd like you to meet Rose."

"Charmed," said Clay, bowing.

"I'm from out of town," Rose said.

"Well, welcome to our humble village." Clay spread

his arms like a carnival barker. He was already drunk. "Lovely Westtown. The place so dull its name is a reference to someplace else. I'm Clay, and the guy impersonating Humphrey Bogart is Artie."

"I thought you were grounded." Artie was talking to David but staring at Rose.

David sat across from Clay. "Time off for good behavior," he said, gesturing for Rose to sit. David popped a beer and took a long swallow.

"Where you from?" Artie asked Rose.

"Osaka."

"Vermont," David added quickly. "Osaka, Vermont. She just moved to town."

The person in the hoodie sipped from the bottle. A few dark strands of hair dangled free from the hood. Shapely pale legs tapered to pink flip-flops. "You gonna go to Saint M's?" Her voice was sweet, but her words were slurred.

Signs of intoxication, read the message beamed to Rose's CPU. **Forbidden.** Red halos danced around the beer cans, vodka, and Artie's cigarettes. **No. No. No.**

"Rose is homeschooled," said David.

"Why don't you let Rose answer for herself?" the girl said.

David looked at Clay. "Who brought Ms. Personality?"

"Becks is my sister's friend." Clay glared in her direction. "Hey, Becks, why don't you share the potato juice?"

"How about I don't?" she returned. "And it's Rebecca, *John.*"

"Becks is in a bad mood," Clay said. "She's feeling sexually frustrated. That's why she won't share the vodka."

He went to tickle her, but she batted him away.

"I'm in a bad mood because my ride passed out, and now I'm stuck here with you." Rebecca nursed her bottle. Her body curved in on itself, a closed loop. The arrow in her brain had no one to point to.

"Where is your boy?" Rose asked.

David, who'd been saying something, stopped midsentence. The boys stared at Rose, then at Rebecca, who held the bottle an inch from her parted lips.

"Why don't you mind your business, smartass?" she said at last.

"I'm sorry. I didn't mean to—"

"The hell with this," Rebecca said, getting to her feet. "Nice friends, John."

"She'll be fine," Clay said once she'd gone. "She's just drunk."

"And we're not." David reached for the cooler at Artie's feet. "So let's correct that situation."

"Hell, yes!" Clay shouted.

Rose shrank in her seat—body language communicating regret, shame. David didn't notice. He was crushing a beer can on his forehead. She felt sorry she'd upset the other girl. But David was happy. That was the important thing. The only important thing.

.   .   .

An hour later, Rose had not moved. Her epidermal sensors registered the night chill, but she had nothing to cover up with. David looked warm on the other side of the fire. His cheeks and neck were flush, and ringlets of damp hair clung to his brow. The boys talked loudly and hit each other, laughing. She wished David would put his arm around her.

Artie wasn't drinking. Instead he smoked and stared at the fire, tossing his butts into the flames. Finally, lighting his sixth or seventh cigarette, he said something.

"Hey, red. What's with the scowl?"

"Excuse me?"

"Why so glum?"

"I'm not glum. I'm waiting."

Artie offered Rose a smoke, but she shook her head.

"It's funny, Dave's never mentioned you before."

"We just met."

"Really? Because you seem really close."

She smiled warmly. "Really?"

"You guys hooking up?"

"Hooking up?" Train cars coupling, a fish caught on a line. This couldn't be what he meant. Artie drew closer, sitting beside her.

"Listen." His breath stank like tobacco. "David and I, we share everything, you know? What's his is sort of mine. Because we're best friends. Do you get what I'm saying?"

Again, Rose shook her head. A new feeling bubbled inside her — like what she'd felt in the car, only subtler.

"So tell me, what gets your motor running?"

He reached to touch her knee. A voice came from behind them.

"Hey, Stubb. I know this is a campsite, but go pop a tent someplace else, huh?"

It was Rebecca, cradling her bottle.

"What's your problem?"

"I don't *have* problems. I *solve* them."

Artie stood and stretched. "Whatever."

"Go bond," Rebecca said, nodding toward the others. "If you're looking for someone to grope, try David. He's the one you're in love with."

"Bite me." Artie stooped to grab his pack of cigarettes and headed for the stairs.

"You wish," Rebecca muttered. She took Artie's place on the I beam. "Hey. Sorry about him. He's just a perv."

"Thank you for making him go away," Rose said. "He makes me . . . uncomfortable."

"No surprise there." Rebecca stared through the flames at the other boys, who were having a thumb war. "Look at them. You and me, babe, we're totally invisible."

"What do you mean?'

Rebecca clinked her bottle with one lacquered fingernail. Rose noticed there was a donkey on the label in a bowler hat. A smartass?

"It's all one big circle-jerk, anyway. They think they're oh-so-funny. We're just here to be the audience."

Rebecca's face was heart-shaped, with pretty, tired eyes. A red bird-shaped brooch was pinned to her sweatshirt.

"I like your top. Is that a rose?" Rebecca asked.

"It's a cherry blossom, actually."

"You should tell people it's a rose. Like your name. It's cute."

Kindness, said Rose's brain. **Return the compliment.**

"I like your hair," Rose said, which was true. It was inky and dark.

"My *hair*? God, why? It's just boring black. You're the one with the awesome hair. Mine's just ordinary."

"I've never seen anything like it."

"Well, thanks. I'm thinking of changing it, actually. A little personal renewal." Rebecca ran a finger along a strand. "Listen, I didn't mean to be bitchy before. You seem nice, and I'm sure David's a good guy."

"He's the only one for me," Rose said, and felt a flicker of warmth, and pictured sunlight glancing off steel cabinets.

Rebecca's eyes went wide. "You must be really into him. Where did you meet?"

"His driveway."

"You're neighbors? I know someone on Horizon Lake. A boy."

"Was he your boy?"

Her laugh was dry, flaccid. "Maybe for a moment. But we weren't right."

"What do you mean?"

"I thought we had a connection, but I was wrong."

Rose squinted. "But he was your *boy*. You must *form* a connection."

Rebecca's thin, dark eyebrows came together. "It's not that simple."

Rose shook her head. "That is a difference of opinion."

Rebecca put a hand on her hip. "Oh, really? Well, my friend Willow tried damn hard to *connect* with your boy David, and he tossed her to the curb like a—"

"That is not true," said Rose.

"You think you're his *first*? Sister, there've been plenty others. And that's not opinion; that's *fact*."

"That is not true," she said again.

The arrow connected Rose and David—it was unbreakable, without forks or intersections. There could never be another spoke. Rebecca was either mistaken or lying.

Rose stood.

"Hey, I'm sorry," Rebecca said. "I'm drunk and . . ."

Rose made for the stairs. Up high her satellite connection would be clearer, with no conflicting signals.

David tipped over an empty beer can and looked up.

"Where's Rose?"

Clay was slumped against the steps, asleep. Artie and that Becks girl were gone.

"Clay." David tossed a can at his friend. It bounced

off Clay's sneaker and spun into the weeds. "Clay, wake up, man."

David got to his feet, steadying himself against the wall. He climbed the stairs with his legs wobbling like Jell-O.

"Tilt-a-Whirl," David mumbled "Everybody loves to ride . . . the Tilt-a-Whirl."

"David?"

A pair of new Converse All Stars was a few inches from David's nose. He recognized the pink flowery socks.

"Hey, baby."

"You're intoxicated."

"You know what I like about you?" David pulled himself into a sitting position. "You don't even sound mad. You're just stating the obvious. David, your man, is drunk. Plain and simple." He looked up. Rose stood with her arms crossed, hair blowing across her face. "What are you doing?"

"I was waiting for you."

"Oh."

"Can we go back to your house?"

"Yeah." David surveyed the landscape—dancing trees in every direction. "We just need to find the car. You have, like, a GPS? Thought not."

The pair stumbled through the underbrush, Rose with a hand on David's back to steady him. "I guess this is an OK touch, right?" David said, laughing at his own joke. "Let's keep that hand north of the equator, missy. I don't want you trying anything fresh. A girl could take advantage of a man in a . . . in a state like this."

Finally they reached the car. David made for the driver's side door.

No, said Rose's brain. "David, you can't drive like this."

"Why not?"

"It's . . . forbidden."

David tossed his head back and laughed. "Not with me, it isn't. Come on, I do this every weekend. It's like three o'clock in the morning. There're no cars on the roads, and I'll go really slow, I promise."

Rose didn't move. David climbed into the driver's seat and started the engine. He looked at her through the open window.

"Do you want to walk?"

"I want to be with you."

"Then get in."

They pulled out onto the empty road and inched back toward Route 20. There were no other cars, and David did drive slowly, occasionally listing to the shoulder. The sound of the engine filled the silent space between them.

"Did you have fun?" David asked when they reached the main road.

"Yes."

"Good. Me too."

"Do you think Rebecca is better eye candy than me?"

"Who?"

"Becks."

"Where did that come from?"

"Do you think she is?"

"I don't think she's hotter than you, if that's what you mean. Why? Feeling jealous?"

Rose analyzed her feelings and found them ambiguous. "How do you know when you feel jealous?"

"Jealous is when you see the person you want to bang flirting with someone else. And it makes you feel angry and tough. Like you could tear a car in half."

"I don't feel like that."

"You don't need to be jealous, anyway. You're the only one for me, baby."

Rose put her hand on his knee, not clutching it this time, but squeezing it. No shock, thank God. *She must feel better,* David thought. *Of course she feels better. She's never been fed a line before.*

This is what Rose saw:

The sweep of trees, the snaking road, the pulse of reflectors on the guardrail. Flash. Flash. Flash. And then a blip, something shining in the darkness between two reflectors. It was a front-mounted bike light, trembling on the shoulder as the rider made his slow progress uphill. But the perspective was wrong. Their twin trajectories, plotted in her mind like glowing dotted lines, should not have intersected. The road slipped away, and for the second time, Rose imagined she could die.

There would be no more Rose, no first kiss, not even a third day.

The tires squealed. David cursed. The wheel spun free of his hand, and Rose threw herself over him, protecting his body with her own. A screech, a clatter, and the world spun.

And then it was over, and David was in her arms.

He was breathing hard. His chest heaved against hers in jagged breaths. Rose squeezed, buried her face in his neck, and felt the soft, hot skin of his cheek press against her own. His smell was a mix of tangy sweat and sweet earth. Then, the crisis over, Rose's body charged for a shock. She slid back, still feeling him in her arms as the world snapped into focus.

"Jesus Christ," David said.

The car now faced the opposite direction, the road bathed in light. Something blue lay on the dividing line. A few yards off, a metallic spider was wrapped around the guardrail. The blue thing wasn't moving.

"Oh, God," said David. "That was close."

The engine had died in the frenzy. He turned the ignition, the engine hummed, and he put the car into drive. They began to turn away from the blue thing in the road.

"David."

"What?"

"David!"

He braked, jerking them in their seats. The car was lengthwise across the road.

"There's a *person* out there," Rose said.

"Yeah, that's awful," David said. "Come on, we better go."

"We can't *leave* him here," Rose said. "Can we?"

She faced him. His face was still flush, his breathing hard, but his hands were steady at the wheel. The haze of drunkenness had lifted from his eyes. "Why not?"

Rose had no answer. She asked herself again and again, but the queries bounced back. There was no rule about this in the data banks.

"That's why you don't ride your bike at night on a dark road," David said. "Jesus, Rose. Just be thankful that isn't us, and let's get out of here."

He began to turn the car again. Rose twisted in her seat, keeping her eye on the thing, the *person,* lying out there. Wearing a blue jacket. His (or her) bike twisted around the guardrail like a tangle of shiny confetti.

How horrible to die out here alone. Better to be here, in the car. Better to be you than him.

As they turned, the headlights caught the bicycle tangled in the guardrail, the light glancing off its twisted aluminum piping.

But what if it were David out there?

The person in the road moved. As David accelerated, Rose opened the door and jumped. She landed hard on her wrists. A thousand minifractures cracked like lightning through her limbs, and instantly a million microbots set to work repairing them.

She heard David yell and the tires squeal. The brake lights flashed. In the crimson light she knelt beside the fallen boy with woolly hair and big glasses, who was slowly turning over, moaning.

Charlie opened his eyes and thought it was dawn. It looked like the sun was rising. Then suddenly the weird light was gone, the night rushed in, and he felt like he'd been creamed by a car.

"Are you OK?"

The girl had tumbling red hair. *So, an angel,* Charlie thought.

"I think so."

"You're not dead." Her hot whisper was close by his ear. Through the pain and the chill and shock, her breath on his neck was soothing. Charlie checked himself for broken bones. He wiggled his toes.

"I'm Rose."

"Charlie."

"Hey, buddy, you OK?"

A figure stood a few paces off. His features were hidden in the dark, but the voice was familiar.

"I think so." He raised his head slightly. "Where's my bike?"

The old Huffy was under the guardrail, the front tire a mesh of spokes. Charlie rose slowly. He put his hand out to steady himself, but the girl, Rose, backed away, as if afraid to touch him.

"Can we take you to the local medical center?" she asked.

"No," Charlie said. "I don't like hospitals."

"Do you want a ride home?" the boy asked.

Charlie stretched, cracking his back. What he wanted was an apology, but that didn't seem likely from Mr. Manners. The girl, though, his guardian angel, was contrite enough. She folded her hands as if praying, her cheeks frosty pink like strawberry icing on soft serve. She was beautiful. But the world was full of beautiful girls — girls who went home with guys in fast cars, not guys with busted bikes.

Charlie tried to unlock the front tire from its death grip on the guardrail. The front wheel was destroyed, but apart from a few scratches, the bike was otherwise undamaged.

"That is an old-school bike, dude," the driver said.

Charlie grunted. He wanted to get away, be home in bed, not talking to a pair of drunk rich kids.

"Well, you sure you don't need anything?"

"I'm fine. Thanks."

"OK, then. Have a good night."

The girl, Rose, lingered a moment.

"I'm so, so sorry."

"It's OK. I shouldn't have been riding so late. It was stupid."

He began to carry his crippled bike toward the road, but a sudden pinch in his hip made him drop to one knee.

Rose's hand clasped his, to keep him from falling. Charlie felt something — like tonguing an old battery or chewing tinfoil, a minivibration that rushed up his arm and into his heart. His vision cleared. She pulled her hand away fast, as if she startled herself. They stared at each other, Charlie's hand throbbing warmly, pleasantly.

"I . . ." Charlie started, but before he could finish, she was gone, running back to the car and climbing inside. It was then he recognized David Sun's Cadillac.

They sped off, washing Charlie in red light, which no longer seemed like dawn, but only some asshole's brake lights.

7. The Countdown

The next morning, Mr. and Mrs. Sun took breakfast on the enclosed veranda. Mr. Sun read the newspaper, fuming over the cryptic crossword. Mrs. Sun read a book called *Messages from Beyond* by Roan Oran.

"How do you think it's going?" Mr. Sun said. After twenty-five years of marriage, the Suns spoke in code.

"Well, he was out till all hours last night." Mrs. Sun took a dainty bite of toast. "I heard the garage door at four."

"I thought she was going to keep him in line. Why didn't we get one that shocked him for breaking curfew?"

"I believe it's a more"— Mrs. Sun searched for the right word —"holistic process."

"You're too permissive with him. If I'd come home that late when I was a kid, my dad would have smacked the hell out of me."

"Wonderful. Then he'd wind up like you. Ooh! Look!" Mrs. Sun gestured wildly to a pattern of sunlight refracted by Mr. Sun's drinking glass. Sun spots fell across the discarded business section (which Mr. Sun had thrown down in a huff). She snatched up her pencil and scribbled down the words they touched.

"Evelyn, what . . . ?" Mr. Sun started.

The book Mrs. Sun was reading, *Messages from Beyond,* said that ghosts often use natural elements to communicate messages to the living. "Only once their messages are revealed can the dead pass on!" Mrs. Sun said, writing furiously. "Is that you, Claire?" But the result was apparently gibberish. "'She-is-Age-in-cod-less-oh-5,'" Mrs. Sun read. "Oh, well, I guess not. Never mind."

Downstairs, David and Rose watched a war movie—or maybe a documentary, they weren't sure. David wasn't paying attention. He was doing some personal assessment of his own.

"You don't actually believe that stuff about me being crazy or whatever, do you?"

Their eyes met. Rose's eyelashes were dark and heavy. Her perfume was like soap and fresh flowers. It might have been a romantic moment.

"I mean, that's why I'm *here,* David. . . ." Her voice was soft, comforting, which only aggravated him more.

Last night was a blur. David barely remembered stumbling upstairs, collapsing on the bed, and waking up again at five feeling as if someone had sandblasted his larynx. He'd knocked on Rose's door around ten to find her already up and dressed, a family of paper birds littering her bedspread.

"But you don't think that's *true,* do you? I mean, Jesus, I'm perfectly normal. I'm like every other kid."

David went to the minibar. There was no booze, only soft drinks. He popped one open.

"Don't be angry." He heard regret in her voice, and fear. *The guilt-trip protocol,* David thought. He stood with his back to her, watching the cola foam. It looked like boiling black tar.

Rose stood behind him. "Maybe you're right. Either way, we get to be friends."

She put a hand on his shoulder, making him flinch. But her touch, when it didn't burn, was so soothing. He turned to face her and remembered that they were alone in the basement, with his parents upstairs. He leaned forward, eyes closed. Her breath was wet and warm. He kept diving, down and down, wondering when they'd make contact and thinking, *Houston, we have a problem.* When he opened his eyes, he saw Rose leaning back. Her lips were parted and her eyes had that sleepy-hungry look, but she was tipped so far back it looked like she would topple over.

"What?"

"I'm sorry."

"Not yet? When?"

"Soon."

"But not now."

She shook her head.

"So, what? Like a few days?"

Rose made a motion with her thumb — not a thumbs-up. She meant *more*.

"A week? Two weeks?"

She tipped her hand back and forth like *so-so*.

"A *month*?"

"Maybe. Probably. It depends."

"Jesus, Rose! What are we, in the 1950s?"

"It's what's healthy. . . ."

"By whose definition? I don't even think my parents would *care* if we were kissing right now."

"Just be patient, please!" It was the first time he'd heard her raise her voice, and he was surprised by how shrill it was.

"How's this supposed to be a healthy relationship if neither of us gets what we want?"

"Perhaps it's about *not* getting what you want all the time."

"That's stupid. I never heard such a ridiculous thing."

He dropped onto the couch. On-screen some heads were blown off, and David thought, *Good*.

Rose sat beside him. "Only one month. We can wait until then, right?"

"We don't have much choice."

She put her hand on his thigh, and David thought of last night in the car, going so fast it was hard to breathe. She shifted, her hand moving just a quarter inch north. She brought her lips to his ear. "Soon, I promise."

Her warm curviness settled next to him. She took his arm and positioned it around her shoulder.

One month, David thought. *OK.*

One month he could handle. He could do one month.

And so began the countdown.

Every day David came home around three. Rose heard his bike pull in, heard him bound up the back steps, heard him coming down the hall. And when he exploded through the door and flung his arms wide, she jumped and ran for him, wrapping her arms around his waist and burying her face in his neck.

"Another day down."

"Do you want to mark it on the calendar?"

They'd pinned a calendar to her wall and crossed off a box for every day they spent together. There was no set date when Rose's body would let her kiss him. The more time passed, the better they knew each other, the sooner it would happen. But it was exciting to see the rows of crossed boxes and feel the moment drawing closer.

In the evenings they watched TV or went for a ride. This was one of their differences of opinion: David loved car rides; Rose did not. She didn't like the flashing reflectors, which made her think of a crumpled blue jacket in the road. But she smiled anyway and kept her hand on his knee.

She asked him about his day, but David usually had little to tell. School was boring — he just sat in front of a monitor all day. This puzzled Rose, since he sat in front of a monitor at home, too. He liked to surf the Web, chat with friends, and read blogs. Rose decided the difference must be her, since he was alone at school, but at home they were together.

They watched movies. David preferred action, but Rose loved romances. She liked comparing herself and David to the couples on-screen. She recognized the longing looks in their eyes, and even though Rose had never stood in the fog while a plane idled nearby, she knew what the lady in the gray hat must be feeling, having to leave her man. And even though David had never thrown pebbles at her window, she knew what it must feel like to throw open the curtains and run down to meet your beloved on the frosty morning lawn. And of course, every movie ended with a long, passionate kiss.

At night, when the movie was over, they lay in David's bed. This was the best part of Rose's day, when it was just the two of them. Talking or not talking. Just breathing. Then Mrs. Sun would knock on the door (which they had to keep open) and say it was time for Rose to go to her own room. They shared a "faux kiss" good-night, which was a trick they'd invented, a way to say "I like you" without really kissing. Rose would press her fingertips to her lips, David would do the same, and then they'd touch each other's lips. David thought it was "so cheesy," but Rose liked it anyway. She was pretty sure he liked it too. It was his idea.

Rose wasn't programmed to keep herself busy during the day, and at first she spent a lot of time sitting and staring. But the longer she was with David, the more things she had to think about and compare with each other, and soon all the activity in her head accelerated her heart rate, and she got antsy. Her hands wanted something to do, and so they made paper birds. Soon her hands got so good at making paper birds they made them without Rose telling them to. When David got home he found more and more on Rose's nightstand, until eventually her room resembled a mini-aviary.

One evening they stood at her window, watching dark clouds move in over the lake. The window was open, and a pre-storm breeze blew through the room. "The air is very romantic today," Rose said.

David chuckled, as he always did when she came out with one of her little Rose-isms.

"Why is it romantic?"

"Can't you feel it?" she said, looking up at him through her lashes. She touched his collarbone, and David felt a crackle, a vibration in his spine.

"Yeah," he said. "I do feel it."

He thought he might kiss her right then, but a cross breeze coursed through the room, and her family of paper birds fluttered up from the desk. Rose made a little noise of delight, but David, unthinking, closed the window and brought their flight to an end. She pouted over the pile of paper, which David didn't understand, but she perked up when he suggested they watch the storm from the covered veranda.

Then one afternoon he found a picture on Rose's wall.

"What's this?" he asked, examining the random squiggles.

Rose was making art, and like all new artists, she hadn't quite escaped her influences. She'd copied the painting in the hall—a dreary southwestern landscape with storm clouds pouring into a river basin, which Rose thought looked like the murky soap Lupe rinsed down the drain after washing the crystal. She'd scribbled circles on white printer paper until the walls of her room were covered with hoary clouds. The differences between her drawings and the soaring vista above the dinette set troubled her, but David's compliments filled her with a new and powerful upward feeling. **Pride.**

He found himself forgetting Rose was a robot. Her diction had changed, become less formal, more easy and fluid. Her gestures and opinions, once painfully recognizable as his own, were blending into a distinct personality, one that was sweet, steadfast, curious, anxious, funny, and *real.* He liked her fastidiousness in the kitchen, the serious way she considered every joke before deciding whether it was funny, her fascination with folded paper, thunder, shadows, and sunlight (Where had these opinions come from? They weren't his.), and of course the way she looked at him, which sometimes stopped him cold, so that he forgot what he was saying.

"You're the best thing in my life," he said once, surprising himself. They were on the back patio in the big chaise lounge, wrapped in a plaid quilt. Their faces were chilly, but their bodies were warm, together under the blanket. David was drinking a Coke and flicking pebbles into the lake. He thought about the sun and how it changed color as it sank, turning a brilliant crimson. Almost the exact color of her hair.

"You're the best thing in *my* life."

He looked at her over his sunglasses, smiling. "I guess I kind of like who I am when I'm with you. I like *how* I like you. Is that weird?"

"I think it makes perfect sense."

He laughed. "I haven't spent this much time with a girl *ever.* I don't think I've been *friends* with a girl since first grade."

"Oh no?"

"Yeah. When we finally *do* make out, it'll be a little weird. Like I'm kissing my sister."

Rose said nothing. Instead she tossed a pebble toward the lake. It fell miserably short.

"I'm just kidding, you know. It won't actually be weird."

"Oh, thank goodness." Rose let out a breath, which made David laugh harder.

"That's my Rose. My Rosy."

"Yo, Sun," Artie called.

David kicked up the kickstand of his bike and watched Artie jog across the parking lot. The cars gleamed in the late-afternoon sun, everything looking sharp and white. Artie shouldered his bag, shirt untucked, tie crooked.

" 'Sup, Artie?"

"Jesus, dude, where have you been?" He stopped a few paces away and coughed. Artie didn't do a lot of running.

"Gotta cut back on the smokes, Arts. You're gonna yack a lung."

"Thanks, Dad." Artie lit up. "So, seriously, I haven't seen you in weeks. I thought we were going to hang this weekend."

"I've just been chilling at home."

Artie blew smoke into his fist, then tossed it to the wind — an old trick. "How's Rose? You chilling with her?"

"She's decent. Yeah." David pretended to adjust his side mirrors. "You know. We see each other now and then."

"Getting to know each other?"

David gave Artie a sideways look. "Yeah, I guess so."

"She touch your pecker yet?"

"Jesus, Artie . . ."

Artie jabbed his cigarette in David's direction. "What's with you and this chick, man? You never used to be prickly about girls. Remember when you taped Stacy Keener flashing you on New Year's and posted the vid on the school server?"

"Yeah, she wasn't too happy about that."

"But you didn't care."

"Well, maybe I do now," David said. "I guess maybe I shouldn't have done that."

"So she *hasn't* touched your pecker yet." David said nothing. Artie nodded. "Yeah, figured as much. Well, damn. It's your life. Just don't want to see my boy get his nuts chopped off."

David glared at his friend, who sniffed nonchalantly.

"OK." Artie puffed. "So when are we going to hang out again?"

"Soon."

"Party at Clay's this weekend?"

"Maybe."

Artie nodded and turned away. Head still bobbing, he started off toward the field, trailing smoke. David tried to think of something nice to say, something to let him know they were still dogs, but Artie turned back first.

"Hey, while Rose is getting to know you so well, make sure to tell her about Stacy Keener," he said, and flashed the peace sign.

▪ ▪ ▪

"What do you want to do this weekend?" David stretched out on Rose's bed, folding his arms beneath her pillows. "Other than be with me."

She tucked in beside him. "I don't know. What do you want to do?"

"Clay's having a party Friday night. That might be fun." Rose said nothing. "So what do you think? Clay's on Friday?"

"OK."

"I'm sure Clay will let us use his room."

"Use it for what?"

"Well, I was thinking maybe Friday would be the night we'd kiss," he said, kissing her hand. "What do you think?"

She smiled into her shoulder. "Maybe."

"Oh, that look!" David said, clutching his chest in sweet agony. He lay back and traced her belt with his finger. "When you give me that look, I think I could wait a hundred years if it meant getting you into bed."

"But you have me in bed right now," she said.

David laughed. "Baby! I think that's your first joke."

"Was it?" Rose blinked.

She was glad he was happy, but she had no idea what he was talking about.

8. The Party

Clay's place was northeast of the lake, in an old neighborhood of stone mansions. The facade was dark, but light and music poured onto a back patio.

Cars were jammed two across on the side lawn. Rose's high heels sunk into the dirt. It was her first time wearing them, but she walked like an expert.

"You look incredible," David said for the fourth time.

She wore her party dress, the calf-length black slip with the slit up the side and the red trim neckline. Her lips were bloodred and her hair was down, carefully styled to fall in waves along the sides of her face.

"What's this theme called again?"

"Pinup," Rose said.

They moved arm in arm across the drive, David in his starched yellow shirt and ripped jeans. To Rose, he looked more wonderful than usual — crisper, as if fresh from the package. She wondered if there were boy Companions, and if they looked like David.

Kids with plastic cups sprawled by the covered pool and on the concrete steps leading to the rear of the house. Rose smelled a sweet smoke, which the data banks identified as **cannabis,** without explaining further. They went inside, where it was filled to the walls with people.

Rose held tight to David's hand as they zigzagged through the party. The air was damp with sweat and cigarette smoke. The music thudded, buffeting them like waves. Someone stumbled backward, spilling her drink inches from Rose. A thick-faced girl resembling Clay was asleep on the couch, one arm dangling over the edge, her mouth open.

"Sun!" Clay called from the kitchen. He wedged between a kissing couple and barreled toward them, pulling David into a bear hug. He wore a jersey with a tie around his flushed neck. There was lipstick on his cheek.

He put a conspiratorial hand on David's shoulder. "Brother, we got some college bitches up in *hiz.*"

David cleared his throat. "You remember Rose, right?"

His eyes moved over her, taking a moment to register her presence. "Hell, yes, I do. Prettiest girl in Westtown. Have a beer." He pressed a dented Solo cup into her hand.

"Now you hold on to that, and make sure nobody puts anything in it. David here is a gentleman, but I can't speak for the rest of these deadbeats."

Rose glanced at David.

"Don't listen to him," he said.

"It's true: don't listen to me. I am thoroughly trashed. Now, have fun, you two."

He smacked David on the ass. He tried the same with Rose, but she ducked away.

"You'll lose a hand that way," David said. "Seriously."

Clay laughed. "Classic!"

They moved into the crowd. "People are looking at you," he said in her ear.

"Am I doing something wrong?"

"No. It's because you're here with me."

He led her to the edge of the room, positioned her against the doorframe so they were visible to the rest of the party, and leaned in.

"Fun, right?"

Rose saw other couples doing the same—the girl against the wall, the boy with his arm around her. She slouched and smiled, mimicking them.

"Yes."

A girl in a lavender sweater placed a hand on David's midsection as she passed. "Hey, David. How you been?"

He nodded in greeting.

"Who was that?"

"I have no idea."

"You know a lot of people."

"A lot of people know me." He looked her over. "You look incredibly hot."

Something shattered in the kitchen.

"All right, who brought the cool kid?" Clay shouted, followed by a chorus of drunken laughter.

Rose examined the other girls. She noticed their imperfections, the flaws in their skin, the asymmetry of their faces. She was more beautiful, certainly. They tottered on their heels, had applied their makeup clumsily, and worst of all, were inattentive to their boys. She was a better girlfriend. She felt David's arm tighten around her waist and leaned into its support. She brushed her hair over her shoulder and fixed him with a smoldering gaze.

"Would you rather be here with anyone else?"

"Not a chance."

He kissed her lightly on the neck, sending a thrill down diodes on her left side. Her skin sensors came alive, activated by this new touch. *Tonight,* she thought.

"I'm going to grab a beer."

Rose felt a rush of disappointment. "Oh. OK."

"I'll be right back, I promise."

"OK."

His gaze clung to hers as he backed away. He left her tingling in the door frame, her locks popping open, one by one, like buttons.

. . .

The keg was in the kitchen.

Three girls sat along the countertop, their legs crossed at the heels. They were tall, thin, and blond. Lacrosse players. The one nearest the keg wore pumps with leather straps winding halfway up her calf. She smiled at David. "Hey, remember me?"

He pumped the keg, the beer gushing into his cup.

"Yeah," he said, not looking at her. "Name starts with a *V*, right? Something weird?"

"Vonis."

"Yeah, Vonis."

"So you *do* remember me."

David sipped off the foam. "Yeah, I said I do."

He started to go, but she stuck out a leg to block his way. Her calf was shiny with perspiration.

"So talk to me a little. Who's that redhead you came in with? She's cute."

"My girlfriend."

"I thought you liked blondes."

"I try to keep an open mind."

"Glad to hear it." She was drinking something red in a clear plastic cup. Her breath smelled like vodka.

"Are you going to let me by?"

"Maybe." She bit her lip. David's eyes fell to her mouth. It sparkled with gloss. "Maybe you'll come find me later?"

He took a long, slow swallow. "I came here with somebody, remember?"

"Since when does David Sun leave a party with the girl he came with?"

"People change."

Vonis slid off the counter. She was almost as tall as he was. He felt her arm snake around his hips.

"Bullshit," she whispered. Vodka and cranberry. Heat radiated from David's collar. He thought he must be glowing. Her body felt good, slender and firm. She positioned his hand on her waist and smiled. Her look was open and promising.

"Come on, we don't even know each other," he said.

Her body, which was all slow movement, froze. "What did you say?"

David's heart skipped. "Nothing."

"Are you serious?" She withdrew her arm. "Did you just say, 'We don't even know each other'? What is this, the fifties?" She laughed, a cold sound. Like squealing ice.

David powered down the rest of his beer and tossed the cup. "Piss off, skank."

"You freaking loser," she spat. People looked up.

David pushed his way out of the kitchen, elbowing a freshman to the wall.

"Fag!" she called.

He didn't look back.

"Where's your beer?" Rose asked.

He grabbed her arm, pulled her in, and kissed her. She melted against him. Her mouth was on fire.

"Let's go upstairs."

"OK," she breathed.

The upstairs hall was nearly empty. A girl sat on the top step, crying into her cell phone. A boy in a leather jacket ran a hand up his date's billowing white dress. David pushed in the nearest door, pulling Rose behind him.

It was a bedroom, Clay's sister's, with a canopied bed and a floor littered with clothes. He locked the door. He pushed her against the wall, kissing her neck. Rose clawed him, pulling at handfuls of shirt. She smelled clean and fresh, her skin hot and dry. David felt dizzy. His face tingled.

"Oh, please," she moaned.

She pressed against him, ran her hands up his back. Their lips touched. David's knees dipped.

"Are you OK?"

"God, yes. Do that again."

She did. This time, his lips parted. She opened her mouth against his, letting their tongues touch, making a blue spark. David withdrew, but not completely. It was like tonguing a Duracell — a grade-school dare. He closed his eyes and kissed her again, a proper French kiss. Her soft lips moved against his. She moaned. He opened his eyes again. Her face glowed. It was glowing in the dark. So was his. Their cheeks were translucent, like kids with flashlights in their mouths.

"Jesus." He wiped drool from his chin. His lips were numb.

"Don't stop."

"I can't."

"No," she moaned into his shirt.

"You're not ready yet. You're shocking me."

"But I *feel* ready."

His crotch ached. He adjusted himself.

"It hurts down *there?*"

He clenched his jaw. "Yeah, it does. It hurts bad, baby."

Rose cooed. "Oh, *baby*. I'm so sorry."

"It's like a vise, you know?"

"What can we *do?*"

David thought. "How about a strip show?"

"A what?"

He lay back on the bed. "No touching. Just . . . you. Getting naked. Remember in that old movie we watched, *True Lies?* That one scene?"

Rose tugged at her shoulder strap. "Um, OK. I think I can do that. There's no music, though."

David turned on the clock radio. He scrambled the dial until he found a jazz station. "This is fine."

A low, mournful saxophone dripped from the speakers. Rose turned out her heel and began to move to the melody.

"Is this good?"

"That's perfect."

She leaned against the bedpost, sliding down slowly like Jamie Lee Curtis. "Like this?"

David was going out of his head. His swallowed away the dryness in his throat. "Uh-huh."

She moved close to him, daring their bodies to touch, leaving a whisper of breath between them. The silk of her dress rustled and fell like a black curtain.

"You're perfect."

"*You* are."

She smiled, loving the effect she was having on him. She unclasped her bra and tossed it onto the bed. David looked ready to explode.

"Why didn't you think of this sooner?" She giggled.

"Don't stop there!"

She laughed again. "OK, OK."

She wriggled out of her thong. She felt fragile, feeling the cool air all over. Shameful, her brain told her, but she ignored it. Naked in front of anyone else was shameful. But not him.

"What do you think?"

David stared, slack-jawed. He squinted, then shook his head.

Rose blinked. "What is it?"

He leaned over and turned on the bed lamp. Rose covered herself in the sudden light.

"Let me see," he said, his voice urgent.

She moved her hands. David stared, clouds gathering in his eyes.

"Are you *serious*?"

"W-what?"

"Why didn't you tell me?" He stood and paced across the room. "All this time!" He was furious, his eyes wild. "I mean, *damn it,* Rose!"

She slunk back onto the bed. "I don't understand."

"What was all this for? All this cutesy stuff! All this you and me stuff! Is this some kind of crazy joke?"

"I really don't understand." She was close to tears. "Please just tell me."

"Talk about not getting what you want." He stormed to the door.

Rose snatched her dress and held it across her front.

"What's wrong with me?"

He whirled on her. "Like you don't know."

She shook her head.

"You're incomplete, Rose. You're a Barbie doll."

"I . . ."

He wrenched open the door and tossed one last furious look over his shoulder.

"What a waste of time," he said, and left.

9. Transistors

The next few days were a blur.

"It's not about sex, David. It's about achieving something *real,*" Dr. Roger said.

"Sex *is* real."

"You're too young," said his father. "We weren't going to buy you a blow-up doll."

"Didn't you find yourself forming an emotional bond?"

"No."

His friends were more sympathetic.

"I can believe the bitch cheated on you," Artie said.

"Let her go back to New Hampshire or wherever," said Clay.

"I'm going back to blondes," David said, finishing the last Miller and tossing the can into the woods.

"*There's* our old Sun God." Clay smacked him on the shoulder. "Glad to have you back."

He was glad to be back. He'd be gladder when they finally came and hauled her stuff away.

"You have no idea where she might have gone?" said the Sakora representative.

"No clue," said David. The rep stood there in his suit, staring at David with small gray eyes, waiting for more. When David didn't look up, he finally turned and left.

The only time he felt bad was at night. He woke up, thinking of her, and turned on all the lights. He turned on the computer, the stereo, everything. He wondered where she was and lay there wondering until the sun rose and the sky turned crimson.

He shut the shades. He never wanted to see that color again.

Drizzle pattered on the generator's steel casing. Thaddeus lay on his back in the mud, flashlight in his teeth, looking up at the fried transistors. Somewhere in the woods a crow cawed.

"Is it hopeless?" Charlie asked.

"She's busted real good." Thaddeus was putting on his hillbilly mechanic routine. "Lightning cooked her insides like a backyard pig roast."

The thought of roasted pig made Charlie's stomach twist. With no power all night and all morning, they'd had nothing to eat but cold cereal. He'd kill for some microwaved chicken wings.

"Can you fix it?"

Thaddeus slipped his flashlight into his breast pocket. "We'll need to go downtown this afternoon and pick up new transistors."

They went back into the darkened house. Half-finished board games and incomplete jigsaw puzzles littered the carpet and the scuffed coffee table. Several dog-eared books with busted spines splayed on the threadbare sofa. Thaddeus dropped into his armchair, then leaped up, rubbing his backside. He extracted an ancient Rubik's Cube from under the cushion — this one much easier to complete since half the colored stickers had peeled off.

The weather had stranded them indoors. Charlie's Saturday bike rides and tromps through the woods would be replaced by hours of numbing silence in the living room with his father, who was just as happy nose-deep in a botany textbook as crouched in a bush. Charlie sat on the floor by the coffee table and arranged a few pieces of the *Mona Lisa,* snapping a section of her hair into place. The famous smile was missing, and Charlie suspected the pieces had been lost since he was in diapers.

"So, what are you doing today?" Thaddeus asked.

"I was thinking of hanging out with some of my friends this afternoon."

This was a lie, of course, but Charlie wanted Thaddeus to think he was being more social.

"Oh, really? Like who?"

"Guys from school."

"Well, that's new. I'm glad to hear it."

Thaddeus selected an old copy of *Botanica* from a pile.

"Does that mean I can stop going to counseling?"

Thaddeus peered over his magazine. "Hey, buddy, I know you don't want to go. But the school thinks it's best, and frankly, I'm inclined to agree. Even if the doctor did prescribe that ridiculous toy."

He meant the Sakora doll. Like a good patient, Charlie had shown his father the catalog. But at first Thaddeus hadn't found it as silly as Charlie expected. Instead he flipped through the shiny pages, pulling at his beard. He even did some research (deigning to use the computers at the town library) and found a few things they didn't put in the catalog — about how these Companions were a limited release, currently being tested on the market in Japan and New England (over the past year in Shrewsbury and Worcester, Massachusetts), how the FDA had been on the fence until Sakora agreed to remove the "girl parts." Holding hands and kissing were fine, but the US government balked at underage boys having intercourse with machines.

In the end Thaddeus said the whole thing was crazy, much to Charlie's relief. *Girls* were hard enough to fathom, let alone ones built to order. As a trade-off he had to have a "check-in" with Dr. Roger every two weeks, a compromise Charlie could live with.

"You know you can always talk to me," Thaddeus said. "But I know there are some things that aren't easy to talk to your dad about, you know?"

Charlie fiddled with an errant puzzle piece. "Like what?"

"Well. Like girls, maybe? You know, real ones?"

"Thanks." *But no thanks,* Charlie thought. It would be a long time before he could hear the word *date* and not smell soy sauce.

"Listen, I know you don't want to be cooped up all day. Why don't you ride into town and get the parts we need?"

"The shop won't open till ten."

"Well, get some coffee downtown. Something hot to eat. Here." He produced a wad of tattered bills. "Don't spend it all in one place."

"I'll try. Thanks, Dad."

Thaddeus parented the way he studied: with careful, loving, detached observation. Food and water, plenty of good sunlight, and the occasional support to help the stalks climb.

Charlie rode the mile and a half south toward the end of the lake where their little street met Horizon Road, the spokes of his new wheel flashing. The roads were slick and black, littered with fallen pine needles. He passed the occasional car, mostly cleaning ladies and landscapers driving to work at the lake houses. Occasionally a housewife in an expensive minivan zipped past in the other direction, onboard televisions blinking away to entertain her kids.

Westtown boasted a historic district preserved to look like the set of *Leave It to Beaver.* The modern coffee shops, Internet cafés, and Apple store all had regulation wooden storefronts, hanging signs, and whitewashed benches out front.

Inside Land's Lunch Counter it was warm, the air filled with the smell of comfort food and the soothing metallic clink of silverware. Charlie sat beneath the black-and-white picture of the Hollywood sign, taken in 1932, when it read HOLLYWOODLAND. The waitress (Peg, according to her name tag) wore skull-shaped earrings. She brought Charlie a floppy fried-egg sandwich and a coffee.

He was halfway through his second cup when a gust of wind coursed through and a trio of girls breezed in. (*Breeze,* Charlie thought. Wasn't that how beautiful girls got everywhere? On tinkling little zephyrs.) They sat across the aisle — Saint Mary's girls, by the look of them. They had long, straight hair and pastel tops, like paper dolls from the same set. Two wore red robin brooches. He'd seen those before but couldn't remember where. Maybe in a play, he thought, scratching a phantom itch on his shoulder. They laughed and chatted, hands flitting, completely ignoring him, even when he dropped his change, as if a soundproof barrier separated one half of the diner from the other. He finished his coffee. It was suddenly too warm, and he couldn't stand that grumbling radio.

He jogged across the street to the tech shop. The skinny clerk found a pair of transistors in the back, so old the price sticker had worn off. He estimated their worth—"Like, two bucks?"—and Charlie tucked the little box with its crumpled corners into his jacket.

On the ride home, it began to sprinkle. Icy drops stung his face and hands. At the fork, Charlie bore left, deciding to circle the lake. He thought about the girls in the diner. He thought about his dad. He thought about the leaves floating on the surface of the puddles, too insubstantial even to sink.

Charlie pedaled past the big houses, up to Cliff Road, which followed the ledge that rose around the northern tip of the lake. His legs burned as he made his way slowly up the incline. One foot down, then the other. The old gears strained and squealed. The black water shimmered in the rain.

He was about thirty yards from the tip of the lake when he saw it—a flash of crimson amid the gray. At first he thought it must be someone stopping to enjoy the view, but as Charlie drew close he could see she was on the wrong side of the guardrail, standing on the lip of rock. A jumper.

Charlie stopped pedaling. She was young, his age maybe, some overdramatic rich girl who didn't get a pony for her sweet sixteenth. The wind caught her hair and tossed it like a candle flame. Her dress fluttered.

"Hey," he called. His voice came back to him, made flat by the rocks and water. *Hey!*

The girl looked up, her eyes dead and distant. Charlie climbed off his bike, letting it fall.

"Wait a second!" The echo came back. *Wait a second!*

His sneakers slapped the wet pavement. He could feel his heart in his throat, and behind his eyes. His breath came thin and hard, like steel. *Oh, God, don't let her jump. Please don't let her jump.*

"Wait!" *Wait!*

She looked down at the water. He was fifty paces away. Twenty. He reached for her as she tipped forward, arms at her sides. His fingers clutched the black silk of her dress. For a beat her weight pulled against the silk and she was suspended above the drop. And then Charlie's feet slipped, and she tumbled forward. He held tight to her. His thighs bumped the guardrail, and then he was following her over, his feet leaving the ground. The ledge came away and the water rose up, sparkling like smashed glass.

And they fell.

Initiating emergency shutdown.

    Please wait. . . .

    David!

    Connection to home server lost.

    LikeSoComeUpToMyRoomLike*Light*DavidRight*yellow*

    Files corrupted.

    Please wait. . . .

YellowBlackgrassnighttreeDavidYellowRedBlue

AI reinitiating.

blueJacketredlight*isShecAge*dawnbirdpapercrimson . . .

Rose.

Booting up senses, diagnostic.

Reboot complete.

Rose felt the icy water all over. She swallowed it, breathed it in. It worked its way into her nose and eyes. Her eyes were open, but all she saw was blackness.

For the first time, she heard nothing.

Darkness and silence.

A hand grabbed her wrist and began to pull.

Charlie pushed up toward the light. It was amazing — the force of life, to the urge to stay living. He burst through the surface, holding her wrist tightly with both hands, and pulled her up, up. She was awkward and so heavy, and he felt himself sinking. But somehow he would make it to shore with her on his back, her arms wrapped around his neck.

10. The Other Side

The room was empty. Rose was alone in the room. Rose was alone.

David had just gone. She was naked, mouth open, breath coming in shallow quivers. The arrow in her mind, unbending, pointed to where David had stood, where now a yellow wedge shone beneath the door. She didn't know how long she stared before her hands began to move. They gathered her dress and sheathed her in its dark silk. She burst into the hallway, bumping a kissing couple, and ran to the hall window, throwing herself against the glass. David's Nightbird was pulling away, onto the driveway and into the night.

"She's drunk," the boy said.

"Dean, be nice."

Rose rushed past them and down into the throng. Her vision was blurring, turning red. **Wrong,** her mind told her. She pushed through the crowd. People stared. **Forbidden.** She was outside, tripping into the mud.

"Whoa, you OK?" someone asked.

Go back. The voice pursued her down the driveway, hammering her temples, turning the world—the world without David—into a smoldering inferno. No more tiny halos. The sky was red, the night burned.

A car's headlights blinded her. A horn blared. She stumbled into the woods, wiping at her eyes. She was lost. Her arrow spun, searching for her boy, but couldn't find him. And every moment away from him was **wrong.**

She felt as if her head would explode. Her mind wrestled with the impossible tangle. She was made for David; she was not made for David. She must **return to him.** She must **please him.** To be with him displeased him. She was impossible; life impossible.

She didn't know how long she wandered. Dawn came with horrible glaring sunlight. How had she ever thought it pretty? She wished for dark clouds. And it was then she came through the brush and saw the still black water and made a choice, her first real choice: to jump.

"Dad! Dad!"

Charlie guided her back into Thaddeus's lab. His father was nowhere in sight. He laid her gently on the couch. There were blankets in the closet. He wrapped her up, letting the water soak into the musty fabric. Charlie checked the thermostat. Dead. The power was still out.

What she needed was heat, hot water. The Bunsen burners ran on gas, but with the power out, he needed a spark.

"Stay there."

Her gaze was empty, her skin the color of fresh newspaper. *Please, God, please don't let her die.*

There was a box of matches in a kitchen drawer. The burner lit on the first try, the flame prancing above the metal tubing. He grabbed a tumbler from the shelf and filled it with tap water. Not big enough to put her feet in, but he could tuck it under the blankets to warm her up. Her breathing was raspy, which could mean pneumonia. But at least she *was* breathing.

Charlie sat on the floor, his face inches from hers.

"What's your name?"

No response.

"Why were you up there?"

Nothing.

"Can you hear me?"

Bubbles rose in the bell-shaped tumbler. Charlie wrapped the hot glass in a towel to keep it from burning her and tucked it by her feet.

"Let me know if that's too hot. But we've got to keep you warm. I don't want you to freeze to death." Words worked their way out of him, like the bubbles in the boiling water. "This is what they used to do in the 1800s, you know, except then they'd use coals in a hot pan. Did you ever go to Old Sturbridge Village? It's one of those historic re-creation places. I learned that there."

One hand fell loose from the blankets. The wrinkled, icy fingertips had flecks of polish clinging to the nails. Charlie stopped babbling. His throat felt full of thick bile. He coughed. At least her trembling had stopped.

A tangle of maroon hair clung to her neck. She was beautiful. And somehow familiar.

"Have . . . have we met before?"

"Blue," she said, her voice almost too quiet to hear.

"What did you just say?"

"Blue," she said again, still staring at the ceiling. "Blue jacket."

Charlie looked down. He was wearing his old blue parka.

"Yes."

"In the road."

". . . yes," Charlie said.

"And I saw you . . . lying."

"Lying where?"

Her words were dreamy and slow, like a sleepwalker's. Maybe she *was* asleep. Or in a trance.

"Lying in the road," she said. "My second day." Her eyes met his, flashing emerald. "Charlie."

And then he remembered. The car running him off the road. The girl coming to see if he was all right. Her red hair.

"Rose."

A smile, just barely visible, tickled the corner of her mouth.

"That's me."

And so they met. Again.

Charlie pulled a sweatshirt over his damp torso. The dry clothes felt good. His skin was chapped and red, as if burned by the cold. Water drummed in the shower. Charlie tugged on heavy socks and tried not to picture the movements of the beautiful naked girl suggested by the changing pitch of ringing droplets.

Her dress lay in a knot by the bathroom door, reminding him of the black leathery seaweed that lined stony beaches. She'd worn no shoes, and her feet and knees had been caked with mud, as if she'd been wandering the woods for days. A half-crazed refugee from a gala event.

Flashlight in his teeth, Charlie shimmied under the generator with the cobwebs and old hornets' nests. He popped out the old transistors, the glass brown and smudged, and replaced them. He crawled back out and flipped the flat switch at the back. There was a noise like something heavy dropping inside the metal casing, and the fan began to sputter and turn. A few cartoonish wheezes, and the generator was pumping again. The lights in the house came on, and he could hear the furnace turn over in the basement.

Charlie threw his hands in the air like a prizefighter.

· · ·

Rose was in the living room, wrapped in a towel.

"Oh," Charlie said, averting his eyes. She was awfully curvy, and that towel wasn't much cover. "Sorry."

She wore Thaddeus's ancient Sony headphones, the thick cord corkscrewing to the stereo.

"These are *wonderful*!" she shouted. "You can't hear *anything* but the *music*!"

Charlie turned down the volume. "Yeah. They're pretty retro."

She removed the phones and ran her fingers along the book spines.

"What are these?"

"Those are my dad's," Charlie said. "Well, some of them are my dad's technical books. He loves them, but they're a little dry for me."

The shower had completely revived her. Her cheeks were pink. She was pink all over. Her eyes were sparkling, though slightly unfocused. Her bare foot tapped the carpet.

She took down a book and opened it sideways, like a laptop, her brow lifting in wonder. She turned the spine so the text was readable, and jabbed the page with her finger. She scowled and jabbed again.

"What's wrong with this?"

"What do you mean?"

"The links don't work."

"There aren't links. It's a book."

She dropped it to the floor.

"What's that?" she pointed.

"A coffee grinder."

"And that?"

"A La-Z-Boy"

"And that?"

"A toaster oven. You don't have one at your house?"

"No, ours was different. Ours . . ." The word hung on her lips. Her toe stopped tapping. She teetered once and dropped to her knees.

Charlie crouched beside her. "Rose! Are you OK?"

"Ours," she said, blinking.

"Whose?"

The clouds cleared from her eyes, passing as quickly as a summer shower. She grasped his sweatshirt, a smile breaking across her face. "Do you have beer?"

"Excuse me?"

"Or cigarettes? I want to try them."

"Uh, no," he said. "Sorry."

"Damn." She bit her lip. "Damn. Shit. Fuck. I *like* swearing."

Charlie examined her eyes. If she was concussed, one pupil would be larger than the other. "Are you OK?"

She stared into the middle distance, not seeing him. "I can do whatever I want! I'm disconnected." She tapped her temple. "And malfunctioning. I'll probably shut down automatically in a few moments."

"Rose, you need to go to the hospital." Charlie got to his feet. "You're concussed."

"That's not what I want," she said. Her eyes searched. "I only want to do what *I* want."

"Uh-huh. . . ." Charlie backed toward the phone. "Just stay there. I'm going to call an ambulance."

Rose stood with purpose. She grabbed his belt.

"Have you ever done this?"

"W-what?"

She kissed him.

In a lifetime of kisses, some must be better than others, and the odds are low — for any of us — that the first will be the best. But few have had a better first kiss than Charlie Nuvola.

He sank into her lips, like an ocean of silk. The smell of her skin, the warmth of her breath, the damp strands of hair that tickled his brow. He felt her breasts beneath the towel, the arc of her hips, the smooth warm pressure of her leg between his knees. Charlie fell apart and dissolved inside her. They were a solution of hair and breath and skin and terry cloth. He floated and dipped and re-formed with every sweep of her tongue, and just as his body completed its transformation from water to fire to lightning to sound, she pulled away.

His lips refused to form words. They'd found a new purpose.

"No sparks," she said.

Charlie shook his head, apology in his eyes.

She smiled. "No, no. That's a good thing."

She kissed him again, opening her mouth. Rose felt him shudder under her touch. She took her time, enjoying herself, experimenting. Her lips lingered on his as she pulled away again, her eyes closed happily. She hugged herself, lost in her own enjoyment.

Charlie shivered. He'd gone numb. "I . . . think I need to sit down." He steadied himself against the bookcase, his thoughts clumping like dough in a bowl. "I thought . . . you . . . uh, I thought you and David were . . ."

The smile dropped from her lips. "David?"

Her eyes tightened, as if facing a too-bright light. Rose fell to the couch and began to sob. Charlie stared, dumbstruck.

That was how Thaddeus found them when he came home.

Rose perched on Charlie's bed. He'd given her a sweatshirt and some of his old jeans to wear. The cuffs bunched around her feet. Her skin still prickled with cold, despite the hot shower, and her neck and shoulders ached. But all Rose noticed was the silence. No voice in her head.

The jump had, as she'd known it would, severed her link to Sakora. The break had wreaked havoc with her physiology. Her emotional center was destabilized. Joy one moment, despair the next, reeling in freedom, then crushed by loss. She was alone, cut off, no sense of what to do, what anything meant, or even who she was. Her body was desperate for touch, yet repelled. She was hot and cold, exhausted but restless.

In other words, heartbroken.

She looked around and saw objects she didn't recognize. Pictures of strange places, a model skeleton of an unidentifiable creature. But when she sent her questions, no answers came back. No one told her to cover up after her shower. No one said she shouldn't sit on a strange boy's bed. Rose was free. But rather than relief, she felt alone. Until now she'd been connected to something, and for better or worse that connection was all she knew. Now she was on her own.

Her feelings were like . . . *water, just before it boils.*

"I think my dad's chill now," Charlie said, coming into the room. "That took some explaining."

"What did you tell him?"

"That you're a friend who's going through a bad breakup." Charlie stood at his desk, afraid to come closer. "That's right, isn't it? You broke up with David?"

She nodded.

"So is that why you . . . ?"

"Why I what?"

Charlie cleared his throat. "Why you tried to kill yourself?"

"I wasn't trying to kill myself." Her eyes ached, as if straining in a glare. She was grateful for the quiet, dark room, and for quiet, dark Charlie. He was so different from David. "But I don't know what I'm going to do without him."

"Well, I don't think throwing yourself in the lake is the answer."

"I don't have a better one."

"What happened?"

"He left me."

Charlie scuffed the carpet with his toe, leaving a track. "That's the worst thing a person can do."

Rose looked up. "Is it? I thought it might be."

"Maybe you could find someone else?"

Rose shook her head. "I'm not . . . maybe some girls can change like that. But I can't. I'm not like them. I'm not normal."

They were silent a moment. It was raining, and the trees shivered silently in the window.

Charlie said, "Listen, I had someone tell me I was . . . not normal. I know how that feels. It feels like a door closing."

She nodded. "Yes, it is like that."

"And you feel totally alone. Cut off from everything."

Rose leaned forward, her hair falling in a curtain around her face. "Yes. Cut off."

She stared at him so intently, Charlie had to look away.

"I'm sorry I kissed you. I was confused."

"That's fine," he said too quickly. "I got that."

"It's a malfunction."

Charlie sucked in through his teeth. "You keep saying that. You know that's not right, don't you? I really think you might need a doctor."

Rose blushed. "I don't need a doctor. I'm . . . a Companion."

The word bounced in his brain, off an old definition that didn't fit. She didn't mean *truest pal*.

"You . . . you're joking."

She shook her head.

Charlie stared. The tension in his body evaporated. His shoulders slackened. He took a careful step forward. Her pale skin *looked* soft, *seemed* warm. He wanted to touch her—for science—but stopped himself. "Can I . . . ?"

"I suppose if I could still shock you, I would have already." Rose blushed.

He took her arm gingerly. He squeezed her fingertips, rubbed his thumbs up her forearm. Her skin felt real, soft and pliant. Even the rigid structures beneath felt like real bones. And yet there was something wrong. He felt hard bumps at regular intervals, and knots of what seemed like wiring at her joints. Where her ears connected to her skull there was a tiny seam, and even her hair itself grew from her scalp in a grid, like a doll's. But only under close scrutiny did she appear to be anything but perfectly human.

Charlie was stunned by the careful, loving detail Rose's creators had put into her features, right down to minute imperfections. Especially the dark oval on the edge of her right palm—a mole. Her skin seemed to be warming as he touched it, and when he looked up, he saw that her eyes were closed. The planes of her face were calm, her lips slightly parted.

Charlie dropped her hand.

Her eyes opened in surprise. Rose breathed lightly, as if startled. Charlie stood. "You're . . . impressive."

"Oh. Thank you."

"It's really unbelievable," he said, staring. "When I saw the catalog, I had no idea."

"Catalog?"

"The Sakora catalog. I got one from this therapist at school."

Rose's eyes widened. "Oh. So you must be disassociated, too."

Charlie looked away. "Well. Yeah, I guess so."

"So does that mean you have a Companion?"

"No," Charlie said, his ears burning. "We . . . I thought it was kind of silly."

"Silly?"

"Yeah. I mean, it's kind of crude, don't you think? Electric shocks?"

"Well, it's not all about electric shocks." Rose fiddled with the sweatshirt's drawstrings. "It's very complex, the relationship that develops. It requires time and patience and an involved understanding." Her features darkened. "You know, it's not like . . . flipping on a light switch."

"So what, you just have some system to tell you how to be in love?" Charlie shook his head. "It's like training a dog. You'd have to be an idiot to—"

Rose stood. "Excuse me, David is not an idiot."

Her tone startled him, but he quickly regained himself. A real girl talking to him that way would have destroyed him. "Well, you're treating him like one, expecting him to learn by punishment and reward."

"We were"—she choked on the word—"*are* in love."

"Regulated lust is not love."

"Why should you know any better? Have you ever been in love?"

Her knowing tone stung him. "I thought you things were supposed to be pleasant."

"Not to *you*."

"Oh, right. Because I'm not your *assignment*."

"If you were, I'd still think you're *rude*." She stood, hands balled into fists.

"But you'd have to *say* you love me." Charlie pointed. "And that would be a lie."

"A *lie*? Then what do you call this?"

"An argument!"

"Well, it's very interesting!"

They faced off in stormy silence, stunned. They'd exploded so suddenly. The air crackled. Her full lips parted, her breathing excited. Charlie had to tear his eyes away.

At last Rose shook herself, ran her hands through her hair, and cleared her throat.

"Thank you for the clothes, Charlie. Good-bye."

"Where are you going?"

She brushed past him into the hall. "Back to David.

I'm sure after a night to think about it, he's realized his actions were hurtful."

"I wouldn't count on it."

She glanced at him over her shoulder, eyes like flaming arrows. "That's a difference of opinion." She grabbed her jacket.

"Fine, go," Charlie said. "You were starting to get annoying, anyway."

"And you, Charlie, are a sour jelly bean."

Around the south side of the lake, cutting through the back lawn toward the house, she returned like a homing pigeon. The damp grass squished beneath her sneakers as she approached the line of privet bushes masking the property fence. Someone was speaking on the other side. Rose approached a small gap in the foliage and peered through. Mr. and Mrs. Sun were standing on the back patio. With them was a man in a suit with gray wispy hair. Their voices were low, conspiratorial.

"Has this ever happened before?" Mrs. Sun asked.

"Unfortunately I can't divulge that information, but I can say that incompatibility is not entirely unprecedented. Our screening process is thorough, but some clients simply aren't suited for the program."

"*Our son* wasn't suited for *your* program?" Mr. Sun crossed his arms. "Sounds like your program doesn't work, period."

"As you were informed, we are still in the trial stages."

"Yeah, right."

"Again, I can offer a replacement. . . ."

"Oh, I don't think so," Mrs. Sun said. "I don't think David's ready for that."

"In which case your money will be refunded as soon as we recover the unit."

"Uh-uh," Mr. Sun said. "I want my money back now."

"Sir, the unit is under your charge, and as your contract clearly states —"

"Listen, forget the money," Mrs. Sun said. "What will happen to her — it — when you recover it?"

The man with the wispy hair took a breath. "She'll be decommissioned."

Rose swallowed.

"You can't . . . reassign her?"

"Babe, who cares?" Mr. Sun said. "Let them sell it for scrap."

"I can't help it. She — it was so lifelike."

Quietly, Rose retreated through the trees, toward the road. By the time she reached the pavement, she was running.

Charlie opened the door. Rose had pulled up the hood to hide her face. Her hands were stuffed in her pockets, and she was trembling.

"Can I, uh . . . can I stay here?" Her eyes searched his pleadingly.

Charlie swallowed. "Sure," he said, stepping aside. "Come on in."

11. Sparks

That evening, Rose sat on a plastic lawn chair and stared across the lake. A glass house lit up the western bank — David's house. The bright yellow lights overwhelmed the stars, but the moon was visible. It was nearly full, a twin orb of light, though paler. Rose remembered reading on the Internet that the sun made the moon glow, and that one side was always dark, hidden in shadow. Tonight, she imagined it was the light from David's house that lit the moon's bright side, making it shine like a silver platter.

She wondered what he was doing. It was eight o'clock. Usually at eight on a Saturday they'd watch a movie. Maybe he was on the computer. Or out driving. She could think of dozens of things he might be doing. It was easy to imagine a new life for David. But not for herself. She knew him so well, and herself not at all.

Charlie was reading on the couch when she burst into the living room. He sat up, alarmed.

"What is it?"

"I'm going to call him."

She grabbed the phone. She'd dialed the first three digits before Charlie's finger came down on the receiver, breaking the connection.

"Why did you do that?"

"Rose, if you call him, they'll come and find you."

"But what if . . . ?"

Charlie shook his head.

"That's sweet of you," she said, cradling the phone.

"You're welcome."

"And also annoying."

Rose went back to her lawn chair. A moment later she heard the screen door clatter shut. Charlie sat in the damp grass beside her, his dark curls trembling in the breeze. The wind rippled the surface of the lake, leaving its imprint like shadows.

"He's the whole universe," she said. "What am I supposed to do?"

"There's more to the universe than David Sun, trust me."

"But he's . . ." Rose struggled to form the concept. "He's *my* whole universe, even if he's not everyone else's." She stared longingly across the lake. She wanted to swim across or jump from the shore and soar to his window. "I wish someone would tell me what to do."

Charlie sighed. "It doesn't work that way. You've got to decide for yourself now."

"But I need him."

"You just think you do. You don't need anybody."

The water gurgled on the bank. The trees rustled. Rose tore her eyes from the lake long enough to examine Charlie's dark profile.

"Don't *you* need anybody?"

"No."

He stood, brushed the back of his jeans, and turned to leave. Then he paused, as if he'd forgotten something. "You're going to ask yourself 'What if' a million times. *What if* I did something different? *What if* I *was* different?"

"So what happens after you ask it a million times?"

Charlie was silent for a moment, then said, "You just stop asking. And you start moving on."

She wanted him to say more, but instead he left, the door sighing shut behind him.

What if he's out looking for me right now?

That was one *what if,* thought Rose. Only 999,999 more to go.

As Charlie came back inside, the door to his father's lab opened. Thaddeus's face appeared in the crack like a rat sticking its nose out of its hole.

"Buddy? Could you come in here a minute?"

The beaker of water, now cold, was still bundled in a blanket at the edge of the couch. Charlie sat down. Thaddeus leaned against the table, arms folded. His face was serious but his eyes soft.

"So. Do her parents know she's here?"

"Not exactly," Charlie said. "She's . . . just going through some stuff."

"I trust you," Thaddeus said. "Just be careful. Maybe you haven't noticed, but that's a very pretty girl out there. And pretty girls who've just had bad breakups can be emotionally . . . just, don't be a rebound, OK?'

"Come on, Dad," Charlie got to his feet. "I'm not anyone's rebound."

"You sure about that?" he said evenly.

"I'll be OK."

"Pretty flowers can be the most deadly."

"We're just friends."

He ruffled Charlie's hair.

Alone in his room, Charlie wondered if he *was* a rebound. Rose was a machine, of course. A replica was just a replica, no matter how convincing. So he really had nothing to worry about. And besides, he felt comfortable around Rose, proof that she couldn't be a real person at all. If she were a real person, he wouldn't like her so much.

The next time Rose heard the screen door rattle, the sun was rising.

Charlie's flip-flops slapped against the wet grass. He was wearing a tattered bathrobe.

"Is your last name Hilton?" she asked.

"Huh?" His eyes were puffy. He looked down at the name stitched on the robe. "Oh, this. My dad got it at a botanists' convention in Boston."

"I see."

Rose turned back to the lake.

"Have you been out here all night?" There was a thin layer of dew on her arms and legs, but she didn't seem to mind.

"I'm up to four hundred and seventy-two thousand, six hundred and forty-one."

"Huh?"

"*What if*s. That's how many."

"Oh." He cleared his throat. "You're, uh, doing them all at once?"

"Yep."

"And how do you feel?"

Rose stretched. Pockets of stagnant fluid in her circulatory system popped and crackled.

"It's pleasant to have a focus." She looked up. "Thank you for stopping me last night. From calling David."

"No problem." Charlie tightened his robe. "I'll be inside if you need anything."

"I'll be here."

The sun passed over the lake. Charlie brought her a sandwich and a CD player with headphones. When the sun was high and the clouds burned away, Rose felt as if her ocular sensors would fry from staring too long. Then Charlie brought an old, cobwebbed umbrella and stuck it in the mud by her chair. Bugs ate her untouched sandwich. As the sun neared the opposite shore, he took the umbrella away and lay a shawl over her knees. He never said anything.

At last it grew dark and Rose stirred, her brain exhausted, sputtering with the effort . . . *like Charlie's generator,* she thought, and smiled to herself.

Inside, Thaddeus was standing at the counter, eating pasta from a turtle-shaped bowl.

"Want some?" he asked, raising a fork of the stringy orange stuff. "I like it cold, but I can pop a pack in the microwave for you."

"No, thank you."

"Charlie's out on his bike. I'm sure he'll be back soon."

"OK."

"Were you really out there all night?" he asked.

Rose nodded. "Thank you for inviting me into your home," she said. There was no voice to tell her **Be Polite To Adults,** but she remembered this was expected.

"Charlie tells me you're getting over a bad breakup."

Rose nodded again. "Yes, sir."

"What was his name?"

Rose began to say it, but got no further than the tip of the D. "I . . . I've thought about him all I can for one day."

Charlie's dad nodded at her over his cold pasta.

"Well, I'm sorry we don't have a television. Would you like to read a book?" He gestured with his fork to the shelves.

"Yes. Thank you."

It was a big collection, but paltry compared to everything on David's computer. Rose decided to read about flowers again.

"Reed's Flora," Thaddeus said. "Are you interested in plants?"

"Oh, I'm interested in everything," Rose said. "The whole world."

She noticed a series of photos in a zigzagging frame on the shelf. In one, a smaller, paler version of Charlie stood shirtless with Thaddeus in a mountain of white fluff. They huddled toward each other. In the background was a still, pearly lake.

"We used to do the annual polar-bear dive at Olive Lake," Thaddeus said. "Have you ever done that? It's pretty bracing."

Rose shook her head.

"Who's this?" she asked, pointing to a dark-haired lady in the neighboring photograph. She was skinny like a small boy and wore large, black-framed glasses.

"That's Charlie's mom," Thaddeus said, rinsing the turtle in the sink. "She left us."

"I'm sorry," Rose said, touching the glass frame.

Thaddeus shrugged, setting the still-dirty turtle bowl in the drying rack. "Not your fault."

Charlie's dad shuffled into the next room, and Rose folded herself into an armchair with two books, *Reed's Flora* and *Anatomy* by James Ried. First it was *Flora,* where *rose* was nothing like Rose, but grown in the ground and eaten by moths. *Anatomy* was more interesting. In the middle a double diagram showed *female* on the left and *male* on the right, the girl and boy holding hands across the seam. Rose examined her page, and saw nothing missing except a black scribble between the girl's legs, which she lacked. A line pointing to this spot labeled it *Vagina.* She closed her eyes, marveling that a few dots of hair were what separated her from David. She brought the pages together so the couple kissed. The next page might have been stolen from *Reed's Flora.* It was a close-up diagram of the *V*-word. Dozens of lines pointed to dozens of parts, connecting them with their proper names. This flower was what he wanted, what she didn't have. Her hand touched between her legs and felt nothing but an intersection with no connection. There was more. Aching, Rose read on.

The sunset was almost blinding, but Charlie pedaled into the glare, up the hill on the north side of the lake, toward the point where he and Rose fell.

Fell. Falling. Falling in love.

He tried not to think of it that way, but he could still feel that kiss. His first kiss. Did it count with a robot?

The muscles in his legs burned. They'd be trembling all night if he kept up this pace. He pedaled hard up the incline and let gravity take him down the other side. He liked that feeling, the momentary weightlessness as the wind whipped by. He rode for yards that way, coasting.

As he came around the bend he saw headlights. A trio of black cars turned from the nearest driveway. It wasn't unusual. At least one important politician lived here, and Charlie had seen his share of motorcades.

But these weren't state cars. In the fading light, Charlie made out the pink cherry-blossom logo.

The cars rumbled by, so close that Charlie had to pull his bike to the shoulder. Sweat prickled on his brow. The third car passed and had traveled only a few yards before its brake lights illuminated. The expensive automobile reversed and came to a stop beside him. A rear window lowered, and a man with wire-thin glasses and hair the color of ash spoke. "Excuse me, could I talk to you for a moment?"

The other two cars stopped as well. Charlie put down his kickstand.

"Shoot."

"We're looking for a runaway. Have you seen a young woman with red hair?"

"How old?"

"Sixteen. She's my daughter, and I'm very worried about her."

A chill cut through him. "I'm sorry. I haven't seen anyone, and I've been riding my bike around here for an hour."

His eyes fixed on Charlie's. The tight black pupils seemed to dissect him like a scalpel.

"Thank you," the man said, and offered a business card. "She's probably near this lake somewhere, so if you see her in your travels, please give me a call."

Charlie looked at the card. Above the phone number was the embossed name. Coleo Foridae. Sounded Greek.

"I will, Mr. Foridae," Charlie said, pocketing the card.

Coleo turned to the driver. "Let's go."

The window went up, and the cars moved out. Charlie could feel his pulse in his throat. There was something about Foridae, the way his eyes dug into Charlie. His bike tires wobbled on the wet pavement.

The caravan was headed north, toward the tip of the lake. There were no more houses that way. The road curved around to the east bank. And there was only one house on the east bank.

His.

He couldn't beat them there, not by bike. But he had to try. Going around the southern shore would take too long. He had to double back and pass them going north, which meant going off-road. Charlie's old roadster had no shocks to speak of, and it rattled and clanged on the dirt paths. Pebbles flew, pinging the spokes. Thicket briars clung to his socks as he pushed forward, breathing deeply.

At the hill he spied the motorcade. They'd pulled over at the fork between Cliff Road and Route 20. Coleo leaned against the rear bumper, cell phone to his ear. That was good luck. He passed the cars and pointed his front tire downhill. There was no path now, just root-buckled ground, spotted with rocks. Charlie cursed Thaddeus for not believing in cell phones. Maybe he could reach her telepathically. *Run and hide! They're coming for you!*

He hit the driveway, gravel spraying in a fan from the rear tire. He jumped off the bike, letting it fall. Charlie burst into the living room. Thaddeus was at the counter, doing the crossword.

"Where's . . . ?" Charlie gasped. His lungs felt full of sand. Stars danced before his eyes.

Rose's head appeared from behind the couch. "Charlie! I've been reading the most amazing—"

"Come on." Charlie grabbed her hand. "We need to go."

"Now?" Thaddeus didn't look up from his paper. "You just got in. Sit down, have some dinner."

"Charlie . . ." Her eyes searched his. "What is it?"

"We've got to go, Dad." Charlie pulled her to her feet.

Thaddeus peered over the paper. "Is something wrong?"

"Tell you later," he called over his shoulder, and then they were out in the night and running.

From the woods behind the house they watched as the motorcade headlights nosed around the bend. The porch light ticked on. Thaddeus came to the front door in his shorts and T-shirt.

"They're looking for me," Rose whispered. Her breath was hot and close.

"Yes."

A trio of men walked up the drive, Mr. Foridae in the lead.

"That's him," she said. "The man who said he'd decommission me."

Charlie and Rose were invisible in the dark, but still Charlie crouched lower. If spotted, they could take off into the woods, but the trees weren't dense enough to get lost in. They'd be caught in seconds.

"What will your dad do?" Rose whispered.

The men introduced themselves. "Please, Dad," Charlie said quietly.

The conversation came in mumbles. Charlie could make out the words *daughter* and *missing*. Thaddeus's face was stony and unreadable. At last he spoke.

"I haven't seen her," he said loudly. *So we can hear,* Charlie thought. "But I'll be sure and keep an eye out. A girl like that, all by herself, she probably wouldn't stay out here after dark. I bet she'd head into town."

Coleo nodded, said something else. The men returned to their cars.

"Oh, no."

Rose tensed. "What? What is it?"

Coleo crouched to examine something on the ground. Charlie's bike. His unblinking eyes rose to scan the woods. They passed over Charlie and Rose, moving in a smooth arc — and jerked back.

"Don't move."

Charlie stared into the gray irises behind the wire spectacles. Coleo turned to one of his men, said something Charlie couldn't hear, and climbed into the car.

"He knows Dad's lying," Charlie said.

"What do we do?"

"Stay away. At least for a little while."

Charlie felt warm pressure on his knee. Rose's hand clasped his jeans. He could see her pale outline, her breath coming like a whisper. Maybe it was just the adrenaline or the terror, but suddenly Charlie felt like he was flying.

"I know where we can go," she said, taking his hand. "Follow me."

They rushed through the trees, their path twisting between the low branches. Rose could hear Charlie wheezing. The adrenaline in her system kept her moving, but Charlie's body was less efficient, and he tired quickly. She slowed, squeezing his hand, pulling him on.

They came through the tree line onto a familiar back road. There was a break in the guardrail and three young trees—*saplings* was the word from *Reed's Flora*—that even drunk kids in a speeding car could recognize in the dark.

"This is it," Rose said.

They hurried down a short path and came at last to the campsite. With no fire burning, the pit was just an open maw, yawning at the stars.

Hand-in-hand they eased down the cement steps. A pink glow emanated from the pit—someone had been here not long ago. The ground was littered with crushed beer cans and cigarette butts.

"Are you OK?" Charlie asked.

"Just remembering."

"Are you sure no one knows where this is?"

"No adults." Rose sat on one of the stone benches. "I don't think anyone will come back tonight."

"Someone was here today, though." Charlie toed a stray bottle. "Hey, look at this." He bent behind a bench and produced a pair of dusty lanterns. The Sun Enterprises logo, a yellow semicircle with a halo of rays, was printed on the side. "Maybe we can get some light." He brought them to the center of the clearing and fiddled with the weather-beaten controls. Nothing. "I guess they're busted."

Charlie sat beside her.

"How long should we stay here?"

"At least for the night. Right? They may be watching my house." Charlie kicked a beer bottle. It ricocheted off a rock and rolled harmlessly into the fire pit. "God, I'm so stupid. Why didn't I hide my bike?"

"You're not stupid."

Rose thought a kiss on the cheek might relax him a bit, but Charlie flinched.

"Sorry," he said when their eyes met. "I'm kind of a wreck around girls."

"I'm not really a girl."

Charlie smirked. "Yeah, well, I keep forgetting."

She took his hand, which was limp and cold. He was uncomfortable, but Rose didn't mind. She was cold and scared, and Charlie made her feel safe. *Like . . . darkness,* Rose thought. *For hiding in.*

"I know you don't . . . you're not familiar with how things work," he said, "between most boys and girls. But you should know, girls don't usually like guys like me. In fact, they never do."

"Oh? Why not?"

Charlie shrugged. "I don't show up on their radar. I just . . . I just don't understand how. How to be around people."

"Why not?"

"Why not? Well, that's obvious."

"Not to me."

Charlie met her stare. His expression was hard. "Because guys who *do know* just act like idiots."

"I see."

"They just try to make themselves look cool or funny. They never say or do anything real. Or honest. And that's not how I want to be."

"How do you want to be?" Rose asked quietly. Charlie was puffing up before her eyes, filled with something hot and scathing.

"I don't know! Just . . . *me,* I guess! But girls don't want that. They just want to laugh and be impressed. So you try to talk to them and they look at you like you're crazy!" He stood, stuffing his hands in his pockets. "It's stupid."

"The girls?" she whispered.

"Mostly."

"And the boys are stupid?"

"Yes."

"And what about you?"

"I'm . . ." Charlie was practically shouting at the sky. "I'm . . . different!"

"Special?"

"Yes."

"So, better."

"Yes!"

His answer smacked against the cement walls and came back to him — a cold, flat echo.

"I mean . . ." he said, his voice softer now. "Not better, I just . . ."

"Gee, Charlie. I'm amazed you don't have more friends."

He stared hard, shoulders rising and falling, until at last a smile cracked the crusted exterior.

"That was supposed to be sarcasm," Rose said. "Did I do it right?"

"Yes."

Charlie sat again. Rose threaded her fingers through his. Charlie didn't change. Charlie was Charlie no matter what. And she liked that.

"You show up on my radar."

He laughed. Rose liked how it rumbled.

12. Pleasure Island

David and Clay sat on the steps of the Peony Pavilion, sipping whiskey from a flask. Inside, dance music thumped. Clubbers went in and came out again to smoke cigarettes. Whenever the door opened, David caught a glimpse of the dancers inside, writhing under the colored lights.

He'd been dancing with girls all night, and his feet hurt. None of them wanted to make out, and when he tried to grind, they pushed him away. He was trying too hard, forcing it. It looked desperate. Now it was late, and the whiskey was nearly gone. Clay tucked the flask into his jacket and burped. "I'm gonna head out. Nothing going on tonight, anyway."

David nodded.

Clay punched his shoulder. "You gonna be OK, D?"

Another nod. Then a shrug. "Yeah, man. I guess so."

David sat for a long time on the steps, slowly sobering up. He was blinded when a car turned into the lot, shining its high beams in his eyes. When his vision cleared, he saw a familiar houndstooth coat and swash of blond hair crossing the pavement. She was on the arm of a tall guy in a baseball jacket—he looked older, maybe in college. David looked away. If he stood up, she'd see him. He slouched lower, willing himself invisible. Then, just as he glanced to see if they'd gone, he saw her walking over, that prim little stride, heels clicking.

"Hey," she said.

"Hey, Willow."

"Fancy meeting you here."

"I know, right?"

She looked around. "Where're Clay and Artie?"

"Not here," he said. "Who's that?" He nodded toward the guy in the baseball jacket, who was checking his voice mail.

"That's Mike," she said, crossing her arms. "He goes to Clark."

"Boyfriend?'

"Sort of."

"Is he gonna mind you talking to me?"

She smiled. "We're not like that. It's an open relationship. We're independent."

David nodded. "Oh. That's cool." It was the coolest thing he'd ever heard. Their age difference had never mattered to him, but now Willow seemed so much older, more mature. Somehow she'd grown up since they'd split, and he'd stayed a kid. It wasn't fair, but it still gave him a hard-on.

"What are you doing right now?" she asked.

"Who knows. The night is young." Actually, he was exhausted, but he couldn't say that. Only high-school kids quit at midnight.

"Do you want to hang out?"

"With him?" David nodded in Mike's direction.

"No, just the two of us."

He shrugged. "Yeah, sure. Whatever."

Willow clicked back to Mike, her hair bouncing. Mike looked in David's direction and smirked. David's cheeks grew hot. What was she saying to him? *Oh, babe, don't worry about him. We used to date, but he's just a kid.* When she came back, she was all smiles.

"You have the Caddy?"

"Sure do."

"Good." She grabbed his arm and squeezed. "Take me for a ride. Then we can go back to my place."

Her place. She meant her parents' house, of course, but when Willow said it, it sounded more adult.

David flew on the freeway. Why not? They were together, Willow and David, the way it was, the way it should have stayed. The two best-looking people in town — it was only natural. How many times had they done this last year? Just zipped all over, taking the curves of 290 at ninety miles an hour, the lights of Worcester flashing by? They drove east toward Marlborough and then turned around and came back. Willow was chatty. She talked about the school play (with a sample of her Cockney accent), her plans for college (she was following Mike to Clark), about how her dad was going to get her a new red Taurus to replace the old white one. It was easy to just listen. *This* was communicating. *This* was connection.

"Do you want to come in?" she said when he brought her back home.

"Sure."

They went in the back door, careful not to make noise—the Wattses were notoriously light sleepers. As they climbed the stairs, David prepared his A-game. They'd probably talk awhile, then get to reminiscing, and he'd say how he'd never found a girl as cool as her, and she'd say she felt the same about him. And then maybe he'd put his arm around her and lean in for a kiss . . .

He was so wrapped up in planning he almost didn't realize they were already kissing. She pressed him hard against the wall, then dragged him to her room and closed the door.

"Mmm." She moaned into his mouth.

No talk, no effort. Just *bam*. Soon they were on the bed. It was hard to get her bra unclasped in the dark, and she had to tell him it was a front clip, not a back. But then he was on top of her, and it seemed like maybe tonight was the night.

"You have to use a condom," she whispered.

"OK."

"Do you have one?"

"Uh, no."

"Hold on."

The bedsprings whined as she stretched for the little table. In the sliver of light from the bathroom he could see her open the drawer and pull out a plastic square.

"Do you know how to put one on?"

"Yeah, I know. Jesus."

David tore the plastic (it took three tries—*shit*, these things were hard to open) and tossed it aside. He rolled the condom down, pinching the tip, like they'd been taught in sex ed.

"Not there. Not there!"

"Jesus, OK. Keep it down. Just . . . show me."

So this is it, David thought. He felt vague warmth, tightness. Nothing special. Nothing mind-blowing. He started to move his hips. She moved with him, cooing softly. Did they have to keep the light off? It was hard to get off without something to look at. He pictured her face, her naked body. Then he imagined other bodies, doing other, more interesting things. His mind unraveled its own cinematic story line until he was miles away from the bed. It was only then he started to enjoy himself.

When it was over, she slipped away to the bathroom. He had a brief vision of her in the mirror before she closed the door. A moment later he heard the shower running.

David pulled the sheets up to his chin. The room smelled like fruit and cigarettes, and like sweat. He was cold.

When the bathroom door opened, his heart leaped. She'd probably want to cuddle, and the thought of her warm body, maybe feeling the thrum of her heart next to his, warmed him.

"All right. You have to go now," she said. She stood in the doorway, wrapped in a towel.

"What? Why?"

"It's a school night."

"Don't you want to cuddle?"

"Why, do you?"

"No. That's fine with me."

He put his feet on the floor and started searching for his pants. He realized he still had the condom on.

"What should I do with this?"

She wrinkled her nose. "Ugh. I don't care. Just don't get it near me."

David wrapped the condom in tissue and stuffed it in his pocket. In the car he blasted the stereo. Let him wake up the neighbors. Who cared? At home, he flushed the wad of tissue down the toilet. As the water swirled, he remembered you weren't supposed to flush condoms. What if it floated back and the maid found it? Or his mother? Was that possible? Funny, they'd never said anything about that in sex ed.

He climbed into bed. It felt good to be under his own covers, in his own familiar darkness. He'd had sex. At long last. And months before his seventeenth birthday. Not bad. And it had been great! He reimagined it all: Willow's writhing body, her moans of pleasure, basking in the afterglow while she showered. It was better to be back in his own bed. The returning champion, the conquering hero. He felt like a man. Solitary. Kick-ass.

David turned onto his side and waited for sleep. When it finally came, he dreamed of a warm body, two hearts beating in sync. Then the alarm buzzed, and it was time for school.

They'd curled up by the cold fire pit. Rose's internal furnace burned off yesterday's excess adrenaline, and when Charlie woke the next morning, everything was covered in frost but them. A damp strand of hair clung to her neck.

Charlie got to his feet slowly. Sleeping on the ground had done a number on his back. Dirt and pine needles clung to his hair, face, and clothes. Judging by the sun, it was early, but he would have to run like hell to make it to school on time.

"Rose," he whispered. Her eyes opened. There was no drowsy blink. Just *bam* and she was awake, like flipping a switch.

"Yes?"

"I've got to go to school."

"OK."

"Stay here, and I'll be back in a few hours."

"OK."

A smile passed over her lips, and her eyes flicked shut.

Charlie ran home. He felt light, agile. He leaped over rocks, bounded off roots. If only he'd ever felt this way on the basketball court. He hit the main road and followed it south to his driveway. He edged down to the shore and made his way to the back of the house.

Thaddeus was asleep on the couch. Charlie mentally thanked his father. No questions asked, he'd bought them time and an escape route. He deserved to know everything. But not yet.

He fetched some clean clothes and his backpack and scribbled a quick note on the whiteboard, promising to explain where he'd been. His bike still lay where he'd left it in the driveway. Thaddeus would probably harp at him for leaving it out overnight.

A thought struck Charlie as he pedaled to Saint Sebastian's. Would Sakora send its goons to school? Would they know to look for him there? The sun was shining, the clouds finally parted. Sakora or no Sakora — whatever happened, he could handle it.

Errant data in Rose's mind, loosed by the broken satellite connection, was sifting, refiling, searching for a home. In human terms, she was having a nightmare.

She lay in an enormous room. She couldn't move, her legs and arms felt stiff and dead. In her peripherals she saw bodies. Hundreds of them. Rows and rows filled the huge space. Men in long white coats paced up and down, taking notes. One stopped near Rose, the wispy-haired man, who now had antennae like a hungry moth. There was no warmth in his eyes, only detached observation. He reached down. When his hand reappeared it held something—her heart. It was a hub of intersecting spokes, slowly spinning.

Rose looked down. Her chest lay open. Inside, flashing red lights, gnarled hairs, and a hole where her heart used to be. She couldn't scream.

Breach detected.
Reinitializing imprint . . .
Please wait.
30% . . . 50% . . . 85%
Imprint established.
David.

Rose sat up, clutching her chest. She was in the woods. The sun was out. Charlie . . . he'd left for school. But something was wrong.

David. The ache cinched her heart. Every synapse, every node in her body rang with it. Being apart from him—it wasn't just pain; it was malfunction, a sin, a tragedy. Her million *what if*s were wiped away.

"No," Rose said, her voice choked and small. "No, I don't want to want him anymore. Please!"

She listened, half expecting to hear the voice again. But there was nothing. Nothing but her own feelings.

Explosions. Light. Rose wanted to pull her hair out and smash herself against the rocks. Even alone, she was divided. How many times could a mind split before it disappeared completely? Rose closed her eyes and breathed. *Please,* she thought. *Please make it go away.*

Something moved in the woods.

Rose's senses kicked into high alert. The sound came again. Leaves crunched in rhythm—footsteps. A large branch lay in the corner. She grabbed it, feeling its steady weight in her hands. "Don't come any closer!"

Someone appeared on the top step. A pair of white sneakers with dangling laces. Strands of dark hair waving in the breeze.

"Oh," the girl said. "What are *you* doing here?"

Charlie pedaled alongside a trundling bus, dust scattering around his legs. Boys in flapping gray jackets flocked like pigeons toward the statue of Saint Sebastian, the red-tipped necktie still snared on the top rod.

There was no sign of Sakora's goons inside. The head hall monitor gave Charlie a long dark look as he passed, and made a note on his clipboard. Charlie lowered his eyes and hurried to his locker. He removed the spare jacket and tie he kept there. A trip to the boys' room to check his reflection (pine needles in his hair) and then to homeroom.

"Hey, watch where you're going, freak."

Charlie looked up, but nobody was addressing him. Instead, George Thomas stood over a crouching boy. The boy struggled to collect his minidrives, which were scattered across the floor. One had landed under Charlie's desk. He handed it back and met the victim's eye. It was David Sun.

"Thanks," David mumbled.

Charlie stared, slack-jawed. The pale, washed-out kid crawling around on the floor couldn't be David. He looked like he hadn't slept a wink.

The first bell rang and the designated monitor shuffled in, looking bored and ornery as usual.

"All right. Eyes down, boys."

Charlie plugged Physics 101 into the port. His gaze drifted toward David, who was holding his head in his hands, looking miserable.

"Sun. You awake?" The monitors had no mercy.

"Yes, sir."

David typed his password and continued to stare at the floor.

"Nuvola, eyes on your assignment."

"Sorry."

But before Charlie turned away, David looked up. It wasn't just exhaustion in his eyes, but something else. A deeper hurt.

No, Charlie decided. You couldn't do what David did and still care. You couldn't throw someone away like an old toy, rip their heart out, leave them completely alone in the world, and then act like you missed them. It didn't work that way.

"What are you staring at?" David said.

"Absolutely nothing."

"Nuvola!" the monitor snapped.

Charlie had no trouble looking away now. He never wanted to look at David Sun again.

At lunch he overheard some boys talking about Companions. One of them, tallish with a hawk nose, drummed on the table as he spoke, bobbing his head to music only he could hear.

"You know, they shock you if you try to grab 'em."

"Yeah," said one with close-cropped red hair. "That's what I heard."

"What good is a sex doll you can't have sex with?" said a third, Luther Drake, who Charlie knew from the basketball team.

"Not even like blow jobs and stuff?" said Hawk-Nose.

Luther shook his head. "Naw, man. Think about it. If they shock you for slapping their ass, just imagine. I heard there was this kid over in Auburn who had his pecker fried."

"Bull."

"I shit you not."

Charlie sipped his Coke. The conversation turned to local politics.

"You at Clay's party on Friday?"

"For a while. You?"

"Yeah." Hawk-Nose snorted. "Hey, did you see that piece David Sun was with?"

"The redhead? From Canada?'

"I thought she was from Maine."

"Whatever, man. I'd fly to the North Pole to tap that ass."

There was general laughter. Charlie began to pack up his things. "Man, she's too good for him, though."

"Yeah, that girl's even out of *Sun's* league."

"Not surprised she cheated on him."

Charlie dropped his change. It rattled across the floor, quarters teetering under the table.

"She cheated on him?" said Hawk-Nose. "How you know?"

Luther shrugged. "David told Clay and Clay told Butkus and Butkus told me."

"Crazy."

"Went down on some guy at the party, I guess — speaking of beejes. David walked in and was like, 'Bitch, we're through.' He left with some lacrosse chick."

"Daaamn."

"Hey, Charlie," Luther said. "You all right, man? You eat something funny?"

"Guy looks like he's about to boot."

Charlie gathered himself and made for the exit. The cold air was like a smack in the face. The wind chilled the moisture gathering in his eyes.

Rose was better at imitating humans than she knew.

"You're David's girl."

Rose lowered the branch. "Becca?"

"Only John calls me that. He knows I hate it. It's *Re*becca, actually." She smiled, pleased to be remembered. "Are you going to hunt for dinner with that?"

Rose stared at the branch and let it drop. "I thought you were someone else."

"Are you OK? I didn't mean to startle you."

"No. I'm fine," Rose said, straightening. "I'm sorry, I'm just not feeling very well."

"Tell me about it." Rebecca brushed off an iron beam and sat. "Seriously. What's up?"

"I think there's something wrong with my brain," Rose said honestly. "I'm feeling several things at once, but they don't make sense together. In fact, they're opposites."

The other girl nodded. "Sounds like you just got dumped."

"Dumped?"

"Yeah, dumped. Like, someone broke up with you. Your relationship ended."

"Oh. Yes. That's what happened."

"David, right? I told you that guy was a player."

Rose said nothing. Rebecca flicked a leaf off the edge of her seat and watched it float to the ground. "I guess I'm going a little crazy, too." She smiled weakly. "That's why I've been taking some personal days."

A breeze rolled through the clearing. Rose thought back to the night she met Rebecca. She'd thought the other girl had lost her boy. Maybe she'd been right.

"How do you do it?" Rose asked.

"Do what?"

"How do you . . . switch boys?"

Rebecca didn't reply. The two girls sat listening to the wind in the trees. Then Rebecca took Rose's hand.

"Come on," she said.

"Where are we going?"

"Let's go for a ride. You look like you need a girlfriend."

Rose knew this term and pulled back. "I don't want to kiss you."

Rebecca stopped short, then smirked. "Not *that* kind of girlfriend."

"Oh."

"Let's go." She pulled Rose toward the stairs.

"But I've got to wait . . ." Rose started. "I've got to meet someone here after school."

"School doesn't get out until three-ish, right?" Rebecca said, setting her cell-phone alarm. "I'll have you back by then, I promise. You don't want to sit around here all day, do you?"

Rose didn't. Especially if there was a chance the man with the wispy hair would show up. "All right, let's go."

Rebecca grinned. "Good. You and me, sweetie. We're gonna have some girl time."

Rebecca's car looked the way Charlie's bike would look if it had an engine and four wheels. The gray surface was spotted with rust. Rose went to open the passenger door, but it stuck.

"Oh, yeah. That door's screwed up. You have to jiggle the handle. It's my dad's car. I've been using it for the past few days because . . . well, because he *hasn't* been using it."

Inside, Rose noticed the emblem on the steering wheel.

"This is a Cadillac?"

"Yep, a real classic." Rebecca turned the ignition. The engine seemed to grind under the hood, rattling the frame.

"David had one, but his was . . . different. It's in pretty good condition." She realized this might have been insulting.

If Rebecca was offended, she didn't show it. "Oh, old Louis here was probably nice once. He's just a little worn around the edges now." She gave the dashboard an affectionate pat. "Isn't that right, Louis?"

The engine croaked in response. Rebecca shifted and turned the wheel, and they rolled through the tall grass back to the road, where Louis's rattling worsened.

They drifted away from the lake toward another part of town, beyond the highway. Rebecca's house sat on the edge of an enormous empty lot. Her house was huge, and Rose said so.

"Forty units in all," Rebecca said, her voice weary. "Buffumville *Estates,* my ass."

They took the elevator to the top floor and followed a dingy hallway to its end. There was a cardboard cutout of a woman in a grass skirt hanging on the door.

"My dad had a bachelor party for his friend Friday night," Rebecca said. "It was tropical-island themed."

The inside of Rebecca's apartment was dank and smelled bittersweet. Shapeless furniture floated on a foamy carpet, and orange light filtered through floor-to-ceiling blinds. A long counter divided the carpet from a tiled floor, where a light buzzed and flickered in an orange casing on the ceiling. Dishes were piled in the sink. In one corner a half-deflated palm tree sagged.

"Welcome to Pleasure Island," Rebecca said.

"Where are your parents?"

Rebecca's jaw tightened. Then her features relaxed and her smirk returned. "Mom's gone. Dad's down the hall. But don't worry. He won't come to until at least four. He's dead to the world, trust me."

Through a half-opened door, Rose saw a dark and cluttered bedroom. A figure lay on the bed, one bare, hairy leg hanging off the side.

"Come on, my room's back here."

Rebecca's room was small, the walls covered with posters of deliriously happy couples breaking into song. Pasted to one wall were dozens of playbills.

"Are these for movies?"

"No, no," Rebecca said, wrinkling her nose. "These are for plays. Musicals. I love 'em. I work weekends at Denny's to save up for shows in Boston. Though they'll probably fire me since I haven't been in to work in two weeks."

Rose sat on the bed. There was a red bird-shaped pin on Rebecca's bedside table. She remembered it from the night they'd met.

"This is pretty."

Rebecca stared at the pin, her smile wavering. "God, don't you think it's tacky? I tried to wear it for a while, but I just can't."

The note was half buried under minidrives and makeup pencils. The visible elegant script read: . . . *our solidarity with the Vogel family, we ask that you wear these brooches in memory of our dear Nora.*

Rebecca began to pry her boots off. "I mean, if you're going to remember somebody, *remember* them." Off came boot one. "Don't just stick a pin on your chest and pretend like that's all there is to it." Off came boot two. "All right, you ready for the surprise?"

Rebecca rooted under the bed and retrieved a plastic bottle. It was identical to the one she'd nursed at the camp-site, with the cartoon donkey in a bowler hat on the side.

"My brand," Rebecca said when she caught Rose's stare. "So, what do we drink to?"

"I can't," Rose said. "I . . ."

Except — she could. There was no voice telling her not to, no dancing halo.

"Oh, yes you can." Rebecca pursed her lips. "Let's drink to . . . to being independent women. Who don't. Need. Men."

Rebecca took a swig, the clear liquid thumping inside the bottle. She winced, wiped her mouth with the back of her hand, and handed the bottle to Rose. The stuff inside smelled like David's garage. Rose took a swallow. It was flavorless at first. But then a second, phantom swallow, this one a fireball, chased the vodka down her throat. Hot coals burned in her stomach. She coughed.

"Well, it's not Grey Goose." Rebecca took the bottle. "OK, what shall we drink to now?"

Rose thought. "Let's drink to . . . breaking the rules."

"Ha!" She took a powerful swallow and passed the bottle. Rose did the same. She wiped her mouth and burped. The girls giggled.

Soon the coal in Rose's stomach spread heat to her limbs and face. The warmth was a pleasant side effect.

Suddenly Rebecca turned somber. "So I've been thinking about that girl a lot."

"Which one?"

"The one who killed herself." She hiccuped. "I didn't know her too well, you know? She must have been so lonely. The night she died I was actually on a date. A horrible date. This guy was so sweet but I just couldn't . . . it was like forgetting your lines in the middle of a show. Does that make any sense? I actually wished I was dead." She studied the pictures on her walls. "What if that happens to me?"

"If what happens?" Rose asked. For some reason she had trouble following Rebecca's words.

"What if one day I wake up and decide I can't be lonely anymore? And I just have to . . . I even thought about taking pills, once, like she did. But I got too scared. I wonder if anyone would miss me. Would it make a difference at all?" Rebecca's already flushed cheeks turned a deeper red. She looked up at Rose from under her eyelashes. "Do you ever think like that?"

"I threw myself in a lake," Rose said. "To stop the voices in my head."

Rebecca squinted. "What?"

Rose put her feet on the ground, which suddenly felt unsteady. Something funny was happening. Colored dots danced before her eyes. Reds and yellows and blues, blending together. The colored lights swirled and flickered. Suddenly Rose smelled mustard. She felt rain on her skin. She saw prime numbers counting down from one hundred.

"I don't feel so good." She tried to stand, but was suddenly on the floor. The landing didn't hurt, but now the smell of cigarette smoke filled her nostrils. Rose rolled over, gasping. A weight pressed on her chest. She was covered in ice. The colored lights were gone, but the smell of smoke remained, combined with onions and bleach.

She closed her eyes, trying to blot out these sensations. When she opened them, Rebecca was leaning over her.

"Rose? Rose?"

At the sound of her name, the smells and the pressure on her chest vanished. Rebecca shook her gently. She was saying something, but somewhere between her mouth and Rose's ears the words were scrambled. Gibberish.

"Rose? Lucky-should-best-now-wait-right-two?"

Rose concentrated, but couldn't find the meaning. "I don't understand."

"You-money-right-stamp-feel-blank-sick?"

Rose moaned and rolled onto her side. The haze began to clear. Rebecca's words shifted back into position.

"Are you OK, Rose?"

"I . . . think so."

"You look like you're going to be sick. Here. Come with me."

Rebecca slipped an arm behind her back, and the next thing Rose knew she was being led down the hallway to the bathroom and lowered onto the turquoise tile.

"OK, here we are," Rebecca said. She gathered Rose's hair into a ponytail and held it away from her face. "Go ahead."

Rose leaned over the bowl. The cool porcelain soothed her enflamed skin. All at once the hot coals in her stomach erupted. The vodka came back out in heaves. It happened until tears streamed from her eyes. When it was over, Rose collapsed against the wall, the hotness drained out. She shivered.

Rebecca closed the seat cover and flushed. "Wowie. I guess you really can't drink, huh? Did you have a stroke or something?"

The room refocused. The sink, the toilet, the solid floor.

"I think I shorted out," Rose said. She shook her head. At least there wasn't any permanent damage.

Rebecca started to stand. "Well, we should probably get something in your stomach. Mine, too. Seeing you heave made me feel kind of *bleh*. Come on. I'll make sandwiches."

"OK." Rebecca helped Rose to her feet. Something nagged at Rose. As Rebecca opened the cabinets in search of bread, it struck her.

"Rebecca?"

"Yeah, girl?"

She swallowed. "What's a sandwich?"

After eating, Rose needed to process her food. She wasn't supposed to do that in front of people, and this was a rule she decided to stick with.

"I'll be right back."

She thought she remembered the way to the bathroom, but the short hallway contained five identical off-white doors. The first led to a cluttered linen closet. On her second try she stumbled into someone's bedroom. It was occupied.

"Oh! I'm sorry."

Rose retreated, pulling the door closed, but had to peek again. A girl stood in the corner, her blond hair falling across the shoulders of her yellow T-shirt, her arms hanging dead at her sides.

"Hi," Rose said hesitantly. "I'm Rose."

The girl blinked and turned slowly. "Hello. My name is Lily."

"Hi, Lily."

Lily stared — not at Rose. Not at anything at all. Her eyes simply looked without seeing. Her voice, and especially that stare, were familiar somehow.

"Have we met?" Rose asked. Of course they hadn't. How could they have? Rebecca was the only girl Rose knew besides David's mother and Lupe, and she would have remembered Lily's startling yellow hair.

Lily cocked her head to one side, her bangs swinging. "We are now at minute two of our friendship. At this point, a handshake is appropriate." She stuck out her hand.

Rose steadied herself on the door. "You're a Companion?"

"My name is Lily." Lily's hand hovered between them. "It's a pleasure to meet you."

Rose knew there were others like her, but she'd never expected to meet one. She'd guessed they were far away, near wherever the voice came from. "I'm like you," Rose said. "I'm a Companion. We're the same."

"How nice. Tell me more about yourself. I am interested in progressing our friendship." Lily's eyes looked through Rose, past her. They were a pale imitation blue. Cold and dead. Rose shivered.

"What's the matter with you?"

"My last diagnostic revealed no malfunctions." Lily giggled. "Shall I make you a sandwich?"

Rose backed toward the door. "I have to go now. It was nice meeting you, Lily."

"It was a pleasure to meet you, Rose. I hope to see you again soon."

The other Companion's skirt was made of a cheap synthetic material with an elastic waist. On impulse, Rose pinched the fabric of the band, careful not to graze the smooth skin of Lily's stomach, and pulled back the skirt. She glanced down. Lily was smooth. Incomplete, like Rose. A Barbie doll.

Rebecca came around the corner just as Rose closed the door.

"Hey, I wondered where you wandered off to. Were you just in my brother's room?"

"I'm sorry. I thought this was the bathroom," Rose said.

"Oh, God. Did you see Paul's thing?"

"What?"

"His sex toy?" Rebecca shuttered. "It gives me the creeps."

"How long has he had it?" Rose asked.

"About two months. They say they're supposed to get more human over time, but it's like *Children of the Damned* in there. How could anyone mistake that thing for a real person?" She put her arm around Rose's shoulder. "Let's watch some TV or something."

In the living room Rebecca folded herself into the corner of the couch and perched a bag of potato chips on her knee. They watched a movie about a ghost in a red gown, leaving clues about her hidden suicide note. Rose sampled the tangy, crispy chips, chewing them into a flavorless pulp.

"So is your brother disassociated?"

Rebecca flinched. "What makes you say that?"

"Isn't that why boys get Companions?"

Rebecca rummaged through the chip bag and pulled out a handful of crumbs. "It's some sort of program they have. The school counselor said he needed one, but we couldn't afford it. Since they're just testing them, he sort of got it on loan."

"Is he nice to her?" Rose asked.

"I don't know. I guess so. He tried to take her to this chop shop, to fix her shocker thing."

"Chop shop?"

"In Worcester." Rebecca crumpled the empty chip bag and tossed it into the garbage. "Apparently there's a place where they'll remove the shocker, so the guys can get their rocks off. Science knows no bounds, I guess."

Rose stared at the television. Pain coiled in her brain, rolling over itself, twisting. She imagined the man from her nightmare opening up her skull and removing it, the dangling, deadly arrow, now kinked and knotted, a confused useless tangle.

"Where did you say this place was?"

Rebecca's cell phone began to chirp.

"That's my alarm. I guess I should get you back, huh?" She stretched her arms and brought her index fingers to her nose. She did this several times and nodded. This was how Rebecca recalibrated, Rose guessed.

"Sober enough," she said. "Let's go!"

When Charlie returned the Sakora catalog, Dr. Roger had asked that he come back every two weeks for a "friendly check-in." The mandatory chats were at two thirty.

"Mr. Nuvola, come in." Charlie took his place in the big chair. "You're looking . . . well."

Charlie looked like he hadn't slept in days, the puffy bags visible beneath the rims of his glasses. Dr. Roger didn't look so hot either. His normally oily skin was the color of ash. He reached for a glass of water and knocked it to the carpet. A little robovac skittered from under the desk to suck up the moisture.

Dr. Roger retrieved the fallen glass and refilled it from the pitcher on his desk.

"So, how are things?"

"Not bad."

"Make any new friends this month?"

Charlie shook his head. "No."

"Come now, Chuck. There must be *something*."

Dr. Roger's unctuous baritone was thinner, more strained than usual. His posture was too stiff, not his usual bored slouch. He clutched his glass, spilling droplets on the carpet. The robovac hummed happily as it sucked them up.

"Are you having second thoughts about the Companion Program?"

A dry chuckle rattled in Charlie's throat. "Not really. It didn't . . ." He stopped himself.

Dr. Roger arched an eyebrow. "Didn't what?"

Charlie swallowed. "Well, it didn't work out too well for David Sun. That's the rumor, anyway."

Dr. Roger pursed his lips. "Yes, I heard about that. I'm sure instances of patient dissatisfaction are rare."

"Doesn't sound rare to me," Charlie said.

"What do you mean?"

"Human beings cheat and lie. Sounds like she was just acting like a human being."

"I see." Dr. Roger took a sip of water. The robovac whirred like a pet waiting for a treat. "And what about you? Any women in your life?"

Charlie had given Dr. Roger only cursory details of his date with Rebecca and had received the "other fish in the sea" lecture in return.

"No."

"Really?"

"Yeah." Charlie coughed into his fist. "Why?"

Dr. Roger shrugged. "You just seem to have a spring in your step this afternoon. I thought maybe . . . but if you say there isn't anybody . . ."

"There isn't," Charlie said, adding after a moment, "I wish there was, you know? But there's not. Not right now."

"I'm sorry to hear that. Well, what have you been up to, then? For instance, last night? What did you do?"

"Last night?"

"Yes. For example."

Charlie's eyes followed the robovac. "I was at home."

"You didn't go out at all? Not on one of your nature walks?"

Charlie coughed again. And then again. "The air is really dry in here."

"I'm sorry. Would you like a glass of water?"

"Please." Dr. Roger filled the second tumbler and handed it to Charlie. "Thanks."

"Anything to make you comfortable." His eyes narrowed. "You know how much my patients mean to me."

"Right. So, anyway . . ." Charlie let his glass rest on the arm of the chair. There was a zipping sound as it slid off the leather, followed by a sharp crunch. The robovac scurried from under Dr. Roger's chair. Dr. Roger lunged for it, but Charlie had the longer reach. He snatched up the robovac, the tiny wheels spinning helplessly. He turned it over. Next to the serial number was an insignia. A tiny pink blossom. The central stigma was a small mesh like a speaker. But no, Charlie realized. Not a speaker. A microphone.

Charlie and Dr. Roger locked eyes. They were posed like wrestlers, half standing, only five feet of Persian rug between them.

"I thought these sessions were private."

"They are private," Dr. Roger snapped. "I'm just doing my job, Charlie."

"I thought your job was to help students."

"Students don't pay." Dr. Roger's voice was a growl. "Who do you think pays for your therapy, Charlie?"

"I thought it was the school." He wanted to sound brave, but his voice quavered. The hand holding the robovac trembled.

"Charlie . . ."

"You gave me the catalog. You probably gave David Sun his. What, do you just go from school to school as Sakora's front man?"

"Charlie . . ." Dr. Roger said again, with something new in his tone. Fear. "It's not like that. I don't work for Sakora, but I agree with their methods, and sometimes doctors and companies can work together." He interlaced his fingers. "I know the lines are a little blurry, but let's just talk about this."

Charlie wanted to say something defiant. He wanted the last word. But he was too scared. He'd never faced down an adult. So he ran. He tossed the robovac and ran for the door, down the hall, and out into the gray afternoon.

He looked over his shoulder a hundred times on the way to the campsite, his bike wobbling on the wet roads. Cars roared past, spraying dingy road water. Charlie imagined black-suited Sakora agents, ready to reach out and grab him. He didn't slow down until he reached Cliff Road and the stand of trees marking the entrance to the dirt path.

There was a rusted Caddy by the campsite. Charlie came to the edge of the pit. Someone was there, text-messaging. Her face was hidden by a curtain of ink-colored hair, but he recognized her.

"Hello."

Rebecca looked up and gasped. "You scared me."

Charlie walked down to meet her. "Hi, Rebecca."

She stood, stuffing her hands in her pockets. "Hi, Charlie."

"Don't you have rehearsals in the afternoon?"

"I quit the play."

"I'm sorry."

Her eyes met his. "Oh, Charlie. You shouldn't be sorry. I'm the one who should be sorry. I was such a jackass, a total pretentious bitch, but it's only because I wanted to impress you." The words rushed out of her, the pressure of days finally released. "Because you're obviously really smart and know science and I'm just a stupid actress with big boobs. But of course you thought I was a total jackass, and I was a jackass. I am a jackass. And I'm just so, so sorry." She took a deep breath. "I'm sorry," she said again, staring at the ground.

"I actually meant about quitting the play," Charlie said.

She covered her face in her hands. "Right. Of course."

Silence. Charlie felt himself closing up. He willed himself to say something. Anything. The first thing that came to his mind.

"Rebecca, I think you're . . ."

"Charlie."

Rose appeared at the top of the stairs, the wind whipping her hair into dancing flames of red. Charlie and Rebecca glanced at each other. Rebecca's smile vanished.

"Oh," she said. "I guess you two are together, huh?"

Rose hurried down the stairs, grinning. "It's so good to see you." She wrapped her arms around him, but Charlie didn't move. Rose backed away. "What's wrong?"

"Could I, um, talk to Rose for a second?" he said to Rebecca.

She nodded. "Yeah, of course. I'm sure you two want to be alone."

"I need to talk to you too," he managed. "If you don't mind waiting."

Rebecca's eyes went wide. "Oh. Um, no. I don't mind."

She climbed the stairs, looking back twice before disappearing above the ledge.

"Do you know her?" Rose said.

"She's just someone I need to talk to." He stared at the spot where Rebecca had been.

"She's lovely."

Charlie's eyes hardened. He faced her. "Did you cheat on David?"

Rose flinched. "What?"

"Did David leave you because you cheated on him?"

"Did you see him? Did he tell you that?"

"Why didn't you tell me?" Charlie exploded. "You just forgot that little detail? And here I am helping, getting in trouble for you . . . and for who? Who are you really? A cheater?"

"No!" Rose said, her eyes brimming with tears. "How could you think that?" She wiped her eyes furiously. "Damn it! Why am I crying? Why is it always me that cries? Why don't boys ever cry?"

"Oh, stop it. You can probably turn them on like a switch."

Rose's hands fell limp to her sides. "Oh. I see now."

"What?"

"You're like him. You're just like him. Is that the way it is with boys and girls?"

Charlie's cheeks grew hot. "Is what the way it is?"

"Boys make the rules. They do what they want, when they want, and the girls just have to be perfect. And if the girls aren't perfect, too bad. They can just be alone. And be lonely. Do you know how awful *lonely* is?"

"Yeah, as a matter of fact, I *do* know." He clenched his jaw. "Look, we don't have time for this. Come on." He grabbed her roughly by the arm. "We have to get out of here. We—"

There was a sharp crack, like a branch breaking. Charlie felt a flash of pain across his cheek. He put his hand to his face—the skin was hot. He gaped at her. Rose stared back, her eyes scared but focused. She'd slapped him. She'd slapped him in the face.

"Don't grab me," she said. He released her arm. "I'm . . . I'm sorry, but you can't grab me like that."

"OK," Charlie whispered.

"I'm *not* your Companion."

"I know."

They were silent. Leaves rustled at their feet. The sting in his cheek felt almost numbing.

Rose sniffed. "I'm not a cheater, either."

"OK," said Charlie. "I don't . . . most people you can't . . . *I* can't trust people, usually. I'd like to trust you."

"I don't lie. And I didn't cheat. But I can't tell you what happened."

"Why not?"

"Because you won't like me anymore," she said. "And you'll throw me away."

"I wouldn't ever do that," he said.

Rose sighed, her breath shuttering. "Companions don't have girl parts. You can't have sex with me, Charlie."

Charlie blinked. "I . . . who said I wanted to have sex with you?"

"Doesn't everybody?"

He laughed weakly. "Well, maybe, but I mean, we're friends first."

Rose didn't reply.

"I like you," he said.

"But I'm incomplete," she said, "and not very sweet anymore. I used to be sweet, at least. I don't know what happened."

"Sweet is nice, but . . ." Charlie laughed again. "You're real."

Rose smiled through her tears. "I thought you were going to say sour." Her smile faded. "I can't get him out of my head, Charlie."

"So, what do we do?"

"I have an idea," she said, sniffing. "But I'm going to need your help."

Rebecca sat on the hood of her car, humming tunelessly to her iPod. When she saw Charlie, she took out her earbuds.

"Lovers' quarrel?"

"Could you give us a ride?" he asked.

13. May Poling

Rebecca piloted the old Cadillac onto Route 290. The late-day traffic was heavy with commuters. The sun blazed behind them, casting a diamond gleam on the city's two skyscrapers.

Charlie closed Rebecca's cell phone and handed it back.

"Well? Did Paul give you the address?"

"Yeah. It's on Water Street. Ten minutes from here." Charlie fiddled with his door lock.

"Could you not do that, please?"

"Sorry."

He looked over his shoulder at Rose, who stared out the window, her expression unreadable. He began fidgeting with the zipper of his jacket.

"You're jumpy."

"It's been a weird few days."

"You'd never know she wasn't real," Rebecca said quietly. "Or, I mean, not human."

Charlie nodded.

"Paul's isn't like her at all."

"She's been through a lot," said Charlie.

"Yeah."

Rebecca pulled off at Water Street, onto the dusty, vacant back alleys. Newspapers shuffled down the street like tumbleweeds. They passed unfriendly doorways and dark foyers, peeling stucco and brick facades, heavily curtained windows and signs for bread companies and hot-dog stands long gone.

"Seven-fifty and a half," Charlie said. "This is it."

Rebecca pulled to the curb.

The building was rail-thin and dilapidated, taking up one half of an overgrown lot between two large warehouses.

"Rose?"

Rose snapped out of her reverie. "Oh. Thank you, Rebecca."

"Any time, babe." She smiled warmly in the mirror. "Call me, OK? We'll hang out again."

"I'd like that."

Rose got out. Charlie cleared his throat.

They spoke in unison:

"Listen . . ."

"Look . . ."

"We didn't get a chance to talk," Charlie pushed on. "I'm not very good at talking to girls."

"You can talk to Rose."

"She's like . . . the only friend I have," said Charlie. "Lame, huh?"

"Well, you should have at least two." He looked at her over his glasses, and she smiled. "Call me, OK?"

"I will."

"Promise."

"I promise."

She rolled her eyes. "You're not so different from most guys, you know." She pushed open his door. "Now get out, ya bum."

Charlie stepped onto the street. He leaned in through the open window. "Thank you, Rebecca."

She smiled, unsure of what to say—then blew him a starlet kiss. "See you around, stud."

Number 750 ½ had a dirty rust-colored exterior. A series of peg-like buttons lined the foyer wall, letters *A* through *Z*. Charlie pressed *P*.

"Yes?" a girl's voice answered. She had a thick Latino accent.

"We're here to see May."

"No one here by dat name."

Charlie pressed the button again.

"Please. I need her to help my friend."

"She no here. Dank you. Good-bye."

"What do we do?" Rose asked.

"I don't know."

"Your friend have number?" The voice came back.

"I'm sorry. What?"

"She have number? On her hand? Your friend?"

"Number on her hand?"

Rose held up her hands. There were no numbers. Charlie looked closely. "Let me see your palm," he said, taking her hand. He examined her mole. If he turned it and squinted . . .

"Yes!" Charlie said, pressing the button. "She has a number."

"I do?" Rose said, stretching the skin. "Where?"

"What her number?"

"It's a one. She's got a number one on her palm."

"Just a one?"

"Just one," Charlie said.

There was a long pause. When the voice spoke again, the accent was gone. "OK, come on up."

There was a growling buzz, and the door unlocked. They climbed a flight of dingy stairs, passed graffitied walls. Empty bottles and Styrofoam cups gathered in the corners. At last they came to the door marked *P.* It was open a crack.

The apartment was neat and white. Black-and-white photos of old buildings hung on the walls. There was a coffee table with magazines, a couch, and folding chairs. It looked like a doctor's office.

Six couples were waiting. Charlie recognized Martin Clark, another sophomore from Saint Seb's, and Derek Fini from homeroom. Derek had his birthmark; Martin a wiry, almost alien frame and gaunt features. The other four, boys Charlie didn't recognize from Saint Seb's, were overweight, pimpled, or pasty. Each was unappealing in some way, but next to each sat a gorgeous girl, a bombshell knockout devotedly stroking his hand, or holding his arm, or resting her hand on his knee.

As they came through the door, a dozen pairs of eyes raised to meet them.

"Oh." The word escaped Rose's lips like a bubble, floating up to the ceiling.

"Let's grab a seat."

They sat across from Derek and a platinum blonde with a supermodel figure, his Companion. She was identical to Paul Lampwick's.

"Hey, Charlie," Derek said. He held his Companion's hand in a death grip. She didn't seem to mind. "I didn't know you had one."

Rose and Charlie exchanged an awkward look.

Derek looked back and forth between them, then nodded. "Oh. I get it. She's brand-new, huh? Yeah. I got mine last week. I'm asking for the full boat. Kissing, touching, everything. Well, I know you can't do *everything* with them. But you can do a lot without a . . . you know."

"What's your name?" Rose asked Derek's Companion. Her face brightened as she turned to Rose.

"Hello, I'm Lily." She extended a hand to shake.

"Rose," said Rose. Lily went back to staring into space.

Derek beamed. "Isn't she the greatest?"

Lily looked like a zombie. All the girls did. The pale brunette holding Martin's arm looked half-asleep. There were only a few models. Sitting across the room next to a boy with ears like car doors was another Lily. There were two identical chocolate-skinned brunettes. Two with midnight-black hair and cream complexions.

Rose remembered her nightmare — the rows and rows of bodies. She hadn't seen their faces, but now she could. Rows of blondes, rows of brunettes, rows of girls with hair like an oil slick. And their names, too. Lily. Others came to her like petals drifting to the ground. Violet. Daisy. Sakora's little flowers. Standing in a row.

But there were no other Roses.

"Is this . . . is this what I'm like?" she whispered in Charlie's ear.

"No," Charlie whispered back. "Not at all."

At the far end of the room a heavy metal door squealed open. A short girl with a black bob appeared. She was dressed in overalls, a tie-dye T-shirt, and loose sneakers. She pulled off a pair of industrial welding gloves and grinned. *This,* Charlie thought, *must be May Poling.* The black-market Companion tech.

"All righty, folks, who's next?"

Derek raised his hand.

May's liquid blue eyes scanned the room and came to rest on Charlie and Rose. Her mad-scientist grin faltered.

"Whoa, hold everything." She was at their side in three steps. "Who is this *vision*?"

"Uh . . ." Charlie said.

"May Poling." She shook Rose's hand. "I'm a Pisces, and very good with my hands. And you are"—she looked Rose up and down—"absolutely *marvelous.*"

Rose's cheeks turned the color of her hair. "Oh . . . thank you."

"Come, you first," she said, pulling Rose to her feet. "You may bring your boy with you," she added, waving vaguely at Charlie.

"But . . ." Derek said. "But we've been here an hour."

"Tut-tut, Mr. Fini. All in good time."

The adjoining room was lined with worktables. Shelves of metallic parts covered the walls. If the waiting room was like a doctor's office, the lab was an auto garage. Loops of wire slung from the ceiling, and clunky equipment beeped and hummed and flashed tiny lights. Some of it still bore faded pink cherry blossoms, though the insignia had been scratched out or, in one case, painted with a red bull's-eye.

"You'll have to pardon the mess," May said. She noticed Charlie staring at her equipment. "Yeah, OK, I took some souvenirs when I quit Sakora. Call it ideological differences. 'Solutions for Life,'" she said in a snotty voice. "As if life was a problem! Please, have a seat. Let's chat."

They sat on a sagging mustard couch. May dropped into a rolling chair and tipped back, propping her sneakers on a bench.

"So the first thing you need to know is that I believe in *choice,*" May said. "I think a girl ought to choose for herself what sort of touching is OK and what isn't. So what I do here, I do for the Companion, not for the dude."

Charlie cleared his throat. "We're not here about that."

May looked at Charlie, then at Rose. "Who's your boy?"

"Charlie Nuvola," Charlie said. "And I'm not her boy."

May raised an eyebrow.

"And she's not my girl," he added quickly. "We're just friends."

"And is that the problem?"

Rose cleared her throat. "I lost my boy."

May's face went serious. "How?"

"He doesn't want me anymore."

May scratched her nose. "Why not?"

Charlie shifted in his seat.

"Because he couldn't have sex with me," Rose said.

May considered this. "Go on."

"I want to know if you can get him out," Rose said. She tapped her temple. "Out of here."

"Ah."

"Ever done it before?" Charlie asked.

Her thoughtful scowl broke into a grin. "No. But I can't wait to try."

Charlie sat back. Rose squeezed his hand. "Um, how much do you charge for that?" he said. "I don't have a lot of money."

"I work pro bono. Or, pro boner, as some of the boys say." She rolled her eyes. *"Boys."*

Charlie shook his head to clear it. He was finding it hard to follow her meaning. "I feel sort of . . . weird."

May leaned forward. "Oh, yeah, don't mind that. You're just a little stoned." She laughed, a tumbling, excited titter. "I'm sorry, I should have told you. It's all thanks to old Bessie here." She rapped her fist against a tin water jug with a thick black extension cord connected to the base. "There's weed up here in the neck. It's calibrated so only the THC burns. No smoke. Just sweet goodness." She favored them with a loopy grin. "Pretty great, huh?"

Rose eyed the dented canister. It looked nothing like Charlie's dad's equipment. "You've got weeds in there?"

Another titter, this one even higher. "Oh, sweetie. We do need to educate you, don't we?"

"Jesus." Charlie rubbed his temples. "It's like there are cotton balls in my head."

May took a dramatic breath. "Yeah, it's pretty good stuff. I can sell you some if you want. . . ."

"No." His words were slow, sluggish. "Just . . . do the thing so we can get out of here."

"Suit yourself." May ambled over. "Stand up, angel. Let's take a look at you." She tugged a flashlight from her tool belt. She was a few inches shorter than Rose, and stood on tiptoe to shine the light in her eyes.

"I don't feel . . . stoned," Rose said. "I mean, I certainly don't feel like there's cotton balls in my head."

"No talking during the examination." She flicked off the tiny light and held it in her teeth. Rose could smell her breath — soda and corn chips. She kneaded Rose's temples.

May mumbled unintelligibly.

"I didn't understand that."

"You won't feel stoned," May said, taking the flashlight from her mouth, "because you don't have those receptors. In fact, you don't have any receptors at all. Your lungs are just a pair of bellows." Her eyes wandered over Rose's chest. May grinned. "Nice ones, by the look of it."

Charlie stood. "I'm going for a walk."

"Bring me back a candy bar," May called after him. "And MoonPies! Bring back MoonPies, too! Poor guy," she said once Charlie was gone. "Some people really tweak out. All right, sister. Up on the operating table, please." She gestured to the high, skinny bed by the window. "Make yourself comfortable."

Rose stretched out. "Will this hurt?"

May leaned over Rose's stomach to adjust the blinds. Sunlight fell across the bed in stripes.

"I'm not exactly sure," she said, scooching a stool to the bedside. "I've never done this before. But it's all the same operating system. Sakora is sophisticated, but not *that* sophisticated. Believe me, I know."

"Are you *sure* you know what you're doing?"

May smiled. Her eyes were like wobbly puddles of blue behind her thick glasses. "Honey, if I can unlock sixty lines of randomly generated code to override the Intimacy Clock, I'm sure I can cure a broken heart."

"There's something wrong with my *heart*?"

May paused. "Sweetness, is your satellite link disconnected?"

Rose looked away. "I . . . broke it. The voice kept telling me to go back to David. So I jumped in a lake."

May scowled. "You could have killed yourself." She sighed. "Still, I can't blame you. Voice in your head telling you everything you do is wrong. I can relate, being a Catholic." She laughed at her joke.

"Thank you for doing this," Rose said.

May slipped her glasses into the pocket of her overalls. Her eyes were small but pretty, the big blue pools shrinking to tiny crystals, fractured by veins of green.

"So here's the deal. I can't just pop open your hood and start poking around with a pair of pliers. It doesn't work that way. Companions are programmed noninvasively, through light and sound. Part hypnosis, part fiber optics, part . . . I don't know, subliminal messaging." She held the flashlight over Rose's right eye, then her left. "Just lie back and think of London, sweetie."

The light began to flash.

"Am I supposed to feel something . . . ?"

"You will. Trust me."

Flash-flash. Flash-flash.

"I don't feel anything."

"Don't look at me; look at the light."

Flash-flash. Flash-flash-flash.

"Just ones and zeros," May said, almost whispering. Almost melodic. "Ones and zeros. Off and on. Left and right. East and west."

Flash-flash. Flash-flash.

"On and off."

Flash-flash.

Flash.

There was nothing but light. The light before life.

Rose heard voices.

"Number?" Husky, low, tired.

"One." High, clipped, familiar.

"One?"

"The first in her series. The first and only."

"Town?"

"Westtown, Mass."

The husky one yawned. "OK, what's the name on the record?"

"David Sun."

"As in Sun Enterprises? Is he the mogul's kid?"

The clipped voice paused. "Yes, I believe so."

"Lucky guy."

"In more ways than one."

"What's the model?"

"A new model." The clipped voice was breathless, full of delight. "She's Rose."

"Very good, Mr. Foridae."

"I'll be watching this one very closely."

For a moment no sounds, just the light, the light that blocked out everything, oppressive, so heavy on her eyes. Light like stone.

"OK. Shall I upload her?" the tired voice asked.

"Yes. Do it now."

The light began to flicker, to flash.

Gasps of black — penetrating, delicious, empty gaps to breathe in.

Flash-flash. Flash-flash-flash.

Breathe, Rose, breathe in.

Breathe in!

Rose sat up, gasping.

"Whoa there!"

May pulled her flashlight away and placed a steadying hand on her back. Rose felt as if a hand had reached inside her — or a pair of pliers — and clasped and twisted and crushed her insides. She clutched her chest, gasping, feeling her heart and bellows and diodes popping back into place.

"What was that?"

"Reprogramming," May said. She eased her back onto the bed with gentle pressure. "Lie down."

"It was awful."

"I'm sorry. I've never seen that happen before."

"I saw . . . light. And heard voices."

"Stimuli linked to the moment of conception." She spoke low, talking to herself. Her fingers prodded Rose's face, her scalp. "Fascinating."

"Did it work?" Rose searched May's face for signs of relief, satisfaction, anything that meant she wouldn't have to go back to that bright place again.

May sat back, hands in her lap. "You're lucky to have Charlie," she said. "He'll be good to you."

"What do you mean?" Rose started to sit up. She wanted to grab May by the overalls and shake her. Force her to say one thing that was clear, that made sense.

"I'm so sorry, baby," she said, taking her hand. "It didn't work. And it's never going to. Not ever."

14. Operation

May told Rose that David was too close to the heart of her. Removing him would be like removing her heart. Clip that wire, and everything would go dark. In time, as more memories piled on top, David would be buried deeper and deeper. She would miss him less and less. Maybe.

May said a lot of things, about how Rose was made, how she functioned. This might have interested Rose on a different day, but today she didn't care. She was going to feel half-dead for the rest of her life — which, if May was right about Companion life expectancy, would be a very long time.

Charlie hadn't returned with the MoonPies.

"He's a sensitive type. Likes to be alone. I can tell," May said.

Rose stared out the window. "Yes. He's special."

"So are you."

"Can I ask you something?"

"Shoot."

"When David first touched me, just a small touch on the shoulder, I shocked him. It took weeks to build up to a kiss. I knew Charlie for half an hour before I kissed him. And nothing happened. Why?"

May leaned back in her chair. Her glasses were on, and as if she'd flipped a switch, the serious edge in her voice had vanished. Her personality was like her eyes, soft and wobbly or sharp and pointed.

"Welllll . . ." She cracked her knuckles. "It could be that your separation from David shorted your security system. Or not. The Intimacy Clock isn't an exact countdown. It depends on a lot of things. How you feel about the person. What you sense about his intentions. What you've shared. Perhaps you and Charlie had a particularly intense and intimate meeting. You knew you could trust him."

"He saved my life."

May mimed a pistol with her hand. "Bingo, gringo. That'd do it."

"You've touched me a lot today," Rose said. "I guess that means I trust you, too."

May smiled slyly. "Yeah, that's the thing. Doesn't work the same for other girls. I guess those Sakora guys didn't think ladies could be sexually threatening." She winked, dark heavy lashes batting behind her thick lenses. "Shows what they know."

Rose smiled into her shoulder. She looked around the lab. It was pleasant there, cool and dark. She guessed it was difficult to work in such low light, especially with defective eyes.

"You're going blind," she said suddenly, not sure of how she knew, but certain all the same.

May smiled. She tilted her head down, and Rose saw a flash of blue crystal.

"It's glaucoma. That's how I get the pot."

"And it's . . . serious?"

May nodded.

The room was quiet except for the contented hum of machines and the soft whisper of May's breath. Rose placed a hand on May's shoulder. She felt the warmth of her skin through the fabric of her T-shirt.

May removed her glasses and wiped them on her jeans. She raised her own failing eyes to meet Rose's flawless synthetic ones.

"I want to show you something," she said.

At the back of May's lab was another door, this one thick, with a keypad lock on the handle. May punched in a code, and it opened with a hiss. Inside, steel shelves lined a small closet, with its single light encased in a glass dome on the ceiling. The closet was empty except for the object on the table in the center — a glass jar filled with a transparent liquid. The thing inside might have been a rare blossom in *Reed's Flora*.

"The epidermis is a latex base," May explained. "The ovaries don't work, obviously, and the womb is, well . . . a little simplified. But hey, that means no periods." She nudged Rose in the stomach. She recognized it from the anatomy book in Charlie's library. She imagined the scientific names connected by intersecting lines—labia, vulva, clitoris, uterus, ovaries, cervix.

"You made this?"

"Yeah." May patted her stomach. "It's kind of my masterwork. I mean, it's far from perfect. But it's modular, so," she trailed off, but then finished her sentence quietly, almost to herself. "So it's installable."

Installable, meaning one could plug it in, add it on. Rose thought of things she'd added to herself—not parts, but thoughts and ideas. Experiences. Everything she'd been at birth—what she wanted, what she felt, who she thought she was—that belonged to *them*. But from that moment on, every decision she made, everything she saw and learned, belonged to a new person. *The person* I'm *building,* thought Rose. *Me.*

"I want it."

May paused before responding. "For Charlie?"

Rose shook her head. Not for Charlie, not for David. She didn't have to explain.

"Congratulations, Rose." May slipped an arm around her waist. "You just passed the test."

. . .

Charlie had followed a deserted street under the highway, past a vacant diner and a dusty lot. He found himself walking uphill by a brick wall, near the Holy Cross track-and-field course. He sat on the stands and looked out over the gray-green grass. A group of girls came bounding down the path in shorts and knee-high socks. They ignored him.

Maybe I'll move to a big city, Charlie thought. *Or another country. Where it's easier to be invisible.*

Thunder rumbled in the distance, and a couple of the girls glanced worriedly at the sky. They jogged around the course in a loose *V* formation. They were long-limbed and sexy. Rain began to patter on the dusty track. Droplets dinged the metal bleachers. The girls were looping back in his direction when Rose came up the path from the gate. She saw Charlie on the bleachers and ran over, her hair bouncing over her shoulders. She stopped a few feet away and pulled it back into a loose ponytail. She was nearly unrecognizable from the spacey android who'd knelt over him that night more than a month ago.

"Hey, I was looking for you."

"I took a walk."

She sat next to him and folded her hands between her legs. She told him about May, about the examination, and about the girl parts May would install.

"Then you'll really be a one of a kind," was the only thing he could think to say.

"Then I'll be like everyone else."

"You'll never be like everyone else."

Rose nodded. "That's true. I'll always be different."

"Special."

"Yes."

"So, better."

Rose chuckled. She put her arm around Charlie, but Charlie couldn't smile. Rose was going to change. She had changed. She was growing and becoming more. And Charlie stayed the same. There was no May Poling for human beings, no one to give you what you lacked, make you a little better.

"Do you think I shouldn't do it?"

"No, I definitely think you should."

The girls on the track ran by, and Rose followed them with her eyes. "OK, then." She nodded, just a tiny little dip of the chin, and climbed down from the stands. "I'll see you in an hour."

"See you in an hour," Charlie said. "Good luck."

"Thanks."

She hesitated, and Charlie wished he had something else to say. It didn't feel like a "see you later" kind of moment. It felt like a good-bye. And then Rose turned and ran across the field, and for a few paces she ran side-by-side with the girls in their pigeon-gray T-shirts before breaking away and disappearing beyond the gate, a flash of crimson.

Rose lay on the table. The sky through the blinds had turned a dusky pink. She wore a loose, cottony robe that tied in the back. She shivered.

"I'm guessing you can't do this with just a flashlight," she said.

May had erected a curtain of pale, translucent plastic around the bed — an antiseptic barrier. She wore a pair of white gloves and a hairnet — what she called her "cafeteria lady" outfit.

"Not exactly." She placed the glass jar on the worktable. Nearby was a toolbox, the contents of which she would not let Rose see, and a complicated rig of tubes connected to a long vertical pole on wheels — Rose's IV.

"I'm going to put you to sleep," she said, adjusting the blinds. "No dreams this time. No visions. A total blackout."

"Are you shutting me off?"

"Yes."

"What happens if I don't come back on again?"

Despite the reassuring pressure of May's touch, Rose's hands trembled.

"It's going to be OK."

"I don't know what I'm afraid of," she said.

May gave her arm a final squeeze and resumed her preparations. A strip of black material was attached to the end of a thick black cord. A sleeping mask. The underside had two nodes, tiny flat bulbs, and when May slipped the mask over Rose's face, the nodes lined up with her eyes.

"Just relax. You'll be asleep in a few moments."

Under the mask, Rose closed her eyes. Soft light pulsed through her eyelids. May hummed to herself as she worked. It was a sweet melody Rose didn't know, and she tried to concentrate on its sweetness, letting it lull her to sleep.

"Twinkle, twinkle, little star, how I wonder what you are," May sang to herself softly. *"Like an eyelet in the scrim, letting little blue drops in."*

The lights pulsed, May hummed, and Rose fell, easily, asleep.

When Rose came to, she was alone. The curtain and surgical equipment were gone. The blinking lights on May's stereo hovered in her hazy vision. It was dark and cool. Music was playing in the next room.

Rose stretched, felt the fabric of her robe move over her body. Something was different. A thrill raced up her spine. The procedure. She pulled aside the cottony material and slipped a hand between her legs. Her fingers felt something prickly. Hair. And then . . .

"Oh!"

The same thrill raced through her — stronger this time. She moved her hand again. Rose felt herself sinking into warm water, light dancing on the lake, the gasp between lightning and rumble. She shivered. No one had told her about *this.*

Outside, in the waiting room, Charlie and May heard her. Charlie looked up from his magazine.

"Is that her? Is she awake?"

May leaned over to the stereo controls and turned the knob, raising the volume and drowning out the sounds from the lab.

"Sit back, speedy. She's not done yet."

Charlie hesitated, then sank back into his chair.

"The way you, hmm hmm . . ." May sang along, quietly, her eyes turning to her magazine. ". . . *buh buh sip your tea . . ."*

15. Grid

The Caddy's doors were open, bass notes thumping through the subwoofer in the otherwise-empty parking lot. Artie and Clay leaned against the hood, a red bag of Cajun peanuts between them. David dozed behind the wheel.

"Yo, Sun, you awake?"

He blinked. Artie's shadow fell across the windshield, blocking the sun's rays.

"I am now."

"It's four in the afternoon," Clay said. He popped a peanut into his mouth, crumbling the shell on the pavement. "Didn't you sleep last night?"

Across the grass, the Saint Mary's lacrosse team was at practice. Their shouts floated on the wind, gusting up to the boys like leaves in the breeze. From a distance they were like a herd on the Serengeti, stampeding in one direction, then another.

David stretched. He couldn't shake his grogginess. He felt raw and distant, as if the rest of the world were behind smoky glass.

Artie brushed the crumbs off his pants. "So she said we should meet up at the Solomon Pond Mall on Saturday."

"This your Internet girlfriend?" Clay asked.

"Yeah, the Viking."

"I thought she wasn't real," David said. The others didn't seem to hear him.

"Damn, I don't know," Clay said through a mouthful. "Picking up chicks on the Web feels lame, but I'd love to get some boob on Thanksgiving break."

Artie laughed.

"Dude, you can't have *some* boob."

"What?'

"You can't have *some* boob. Boob is not a quantity you can have *some* of."

David closed his eyes. The sunlight felt good on his lids, leaving its dreamy orange wash on his retinas. "Haven't we had this conversation before?" he said.

Clay chuckled. "What do you mean you can't have *some* boob? You can have *some* ass . . ."

Artie laughed so hard he spilled the bag of peanuts. It slumped lazily to the ground, dumping a powdery red dust on the concrete.

"You guys want to get out of here?" David said.

Clay retrieved the bag and salvaged what remained. "So tell me more about Viking."

"Her profile pic is pretty hot."

"Nice."

"Guys, are you listening to me?"

"Yeah. Blond, sort of. Like, bottle-blond."

David got out of the car and trudged toward the school. Across the field, a Saint Seb's kid was running toward the lot, waving his arms.

"Davie, where you going?" Clay called. His lips were stained with pepper flakes.

David ignored him.

He went inside. The halls were cool and dark. Someone slammed a locker and the sound ricocheted through the empty corridors, slapping against David's exhausted brain. Muffled music came from the auditorium. Then, the doors David had just passed through burst open and Paul Lampwick, red-faced and gasping, jogged into the hall.

"Da—" he started, and coughed. "Hey, David. Wait!"

"Not now, Lampwick." He shoved his hands in his pockets and walked on, but Paul caught up.

"I just got a call from Charlie Nuvola, from my sister's phone?" He seemed to expect a response, but David said nothing. "He was calling about your old girlfriend."

David stopped. Paul waited for the information to sink in. Finally David turned. "What about Willow?"

"Not Willow, the other one. The redhead everyone's talking about."

David tried to comprehend the improbability of this statement. It was flying pigs, talking bears. Ridiculous.

"They were looking for this place for, well . . ." He looked up the hall to see if anyone was coming. "David, was she a *Companion*?"

David worked his jaw, saying nothing.

"It's OK. I have one, too!" Paul said, stepping closer. "She's nothing like yours, though. She's . . ."

"Shut up, Paul."

"But why's yours with Charlie? Did you, like, sell her or something? Isn't that against the rules?"

"I said *shut up!*" He pushed Paul backward, knocking the other boy into the lockers.

"But . . ." Paul looked ready to cry. "But, we're the same!"

David stalked away, blocking out whatever Paul said next. He felt a tickle at the back of his throat. It turned into a furious mumble, a growl. By the time he reached the stairs, words were forming, a series of half-real, half-invented curses, the gibberish coming out hot and low under his breath. He ducked into the men's room — the one for male faculty — and shouted himself hoarse in the mirror. He yelled at the oblivious stragglers crossing the courtyard out the window, at Saint Sebastian, whose radius of spikes reached out to nowhere, connected to nothing.

Finally he slumped to the dirty tile floor. The close air was clogged with words. They hung like toxic gas, suffocating.

The door flew open. On the other side was Dr. Roger, his eyes wide and curious. He looked like he'd been running.

"Jesus," he said, startled to find a student there. "Was that you screaming?"

David couldn't speak.

Dr. Roger opened the door a little farther. "Come on out," he said. "You look like you need someone to talk to."

David took a long breath, and nodded.

It was getting late; the yellow sun was falling. They'd caught the five o'clock bus back from May's. They followed the path down to the campsite. The sky burned crimson through the bowed branches, which seemed to close over the pit, like eyelashes, Charlie thought.

Rose sat in the dirt and hugged her knees to her chin. Charlie sat too, a little apart. The dead lanterns lolled by the fire pit, tipped toward each other, dark. They watched the sky transition through crimson to purple and finally into pitch night. The moon was full, a shiny dime.

"Was it because of Rebecca that you had to ask a million *what ifs*?" Rose asked suddenly.

Charlie squinted, not sure what she meant. Then a sad smile found its way to his lips. "No, not Rebecca. When I was in the eighth grade, my mother left my dad. And I wondered if it was because of me. I mean, I know it wasn't. But . . . I guess I'll never know, really."

Charlie looked at the sky. Rose looked at Charlie. She threaded her fingers through his and squeezed. "I'm so sorry, Charlie."

He looked her in the eye. "I lied to you. I'm still asking. And I won't ever stop. Not after a billion. Not after a hundred billion. But . . ." He turned so their bodies faced each other.

"I think you'll stop asking someday," Rose said. She kissed the tip of his nose. Charlie took off his glasses and rubbed his eyes. They were a gray blue, almost smoky. They were startling. "Thank you, Charlie. You didn't have to help me, you know."

"It's no big deal."

"You had to run away from home, from school, go to an illegal chop shop. Of course it's a big deal."

"Jesus, Rose, they would have shut you down," said Charlie. "I couldn't let that happen."

Something in his tone reminded her of David—a certainty, and a hardness to the words. But of course, the words were so different, words David would never say. She thought of that night they nearly hit Charlie. *Jesus, Rose. Just be thankful that isn't us.* Charlie was the cloud to David's sunshine. *The dark side of his moon,* Rose thought. Something in her brain twitched. Charlie was the flip side of David's bright spot, the shadow side. The map began to turn, breaking into the third dimension. And her unbending arrow, pointing to David, pointed also to Charlie. It was a feeling, reflected.

Rose felt warmth swell inside—a universe expanding rapidly outward. And suddenly there was room enough in her world for one more person: Her choice. Her Charlie.

"Come here," she said.

And she kissed him.

Electricity crackled. Not electricity that hurt, but a radiating energy. Rose opened her eyes. The lanterns were alive. Burning. She kissed him again, her fingers pressed into his back. Charlie's hands moved over her, her legs, her chest. Different hands, new hands, but oh-so-right hands. The lanterns burned hotter, brighter.

She pushed him gently and lay on top of him. Her hair fell around his face, and he felt her breath on his eyelids, his lips. She kissed him and folded her arms behind his neck.

They stripped awkwardly, until their clothes were crumpled tendrils in the dirt. Charlie's fingertips and toes tingled. His face was numb. He thought he might pass out.

Their bodies connected, a completed circuit. An arc of blue-white electricity jumped from Charlie to Rose and back again, like a ribbon of light. A blue fairy. They were joined, linked up, bound together.

And Charlie had a vision. He saw his town as if from space, and saw the tiny blue dash that was the light connecting him to Rose. And he saw that light jump to someone else, and then to someone else, to David, to Rebecca, to Artie, to his father, to the wispy-haired man. Everyone, all of them were connected by bands of light, and the town lit up like a power grid, an unbreakable glowing web, burning brighter and brighter but not burning his eyes, until it was all light, all of it, everything alive. Charlie's heart fluttered. He was flying, passing through unharmed into all that blue. He gasped.

The lanterns exploded in a shower of sparks.

Afterward, Rose kissed his forehead.

They lay in the pit for a long time, watching the blue stars make their slow arc across the sky, feeling as if the Milky Way shimmered in ovation, just for them. Charlie was too dazed to speak. He felt overwhelmed, spacey, untouchable. Eventually they were both asleep.

There was connection. Everything was connected. And he wouldn't lose her. Not ever.

Charlie rolled over, feeling the sun on his face. He pressed his cheek into the damp sand, and when they were ready, let his eyes open slowly. A silvery moth perched on Rose's jacket, drying its wings in the breeze.

Charlie sat up. The sudden movement startled the moth into flight. He looked right, left, stood. Cold breeze blew through the pit. Tracks in the sand led from the stairs to where Rose had slept. Men's shoes. They'd taken her. She was gone.

Charlie was alone.

He would go to May. May would know what to do. But Water Street was blocked off. Charlie slowed as he approached, coming to a halt by the wooden police barrier. Several cruisers were parked across from May's building, their lights silently twirling. Men in uniform milled around the open door and neighbors hung out of windows, gaping. A small crowd had gathered by the barrier, and Charlie had to crane his neck to see over the taller gawkers. Men pushed handcarts and carried large boxes toward black vans, taking back their equipment.

"What's going on?" he asked.

"A drug bust," one man said. "Or something. Looks like someone was running a meth lab outta that apartment."

He felt something tap his back. He turned. A small person in a tie-dye hoodie stood apart from the crowd. She'd thrown a pebble at him.

Charlie backed away and edged toward May. Her eyes were hidden behind large, bug-eye sunglasses. She didn't look at Charlie when she spoke.

"Not too close. Don't let them see us together."

Charlie was shaking. Somehow he'd made it this far without saying it to himself. "They took Rose. Somehow they found us and they took her."

"Someone tipped them off."

"Who?"

"My bet is the guy in the Cadillac. He rolled up with the fuzz."

Charlie glanced at the pair of police cruisers parked in the far lot. Beside them was a sleek sports car — far too nice for the Worcester police department.

"That's David Sun's car."

May shoved her hands in her pockets. "What does he have against me?"

"Nothing against you," Charlie said. "I'm sorry, May. Your shop."

She shrugged. "It's all right. I can rebuild. They can shut us down, but they can't stop us."

"Could you be arrested?"

May turned to Charlie and grinned. "Only if they catch me."

When she reached the corner she turned, flashed him the peace sign, and disappeared.

Charlie made for the lot.

"David."

The cruisers were empty. David Sun sat behind the wheel of his Cadillac, arms folded. When he saw Charlie, he jumped. The window came down with a whir.

"Nuvola."

Charlie's voice was low, calm. "Get out of the car."

David stared, his face blank. Obediently, he got out.

"Where's Rose?" Charlie said.

"What?"

Charlie shoved David against the car.

"I said, where's Rose!"

David's eyes narrowed. He shoved back. "The hell with you."

"Where did they take her?"

"It's none of your damn business," David said. He grabbed the front of Charlie's jacket and shoved him backward.

"Tell me where she is, or I swear to God—"

"Piss off, Nuvola. This isn't about you."

David turned to get back in the car. Charlie whirled him around and socked him in the stomach. David's eyes bulged. He doubled over and coughed, spitting bile onto the pavement.

"Son of a—"

David didn't finish his sentence; he countered with an uppercut. Charlie's jaw exploded in pain. His feet left the ground as he rocketed backward, bouncing off the police cruiser and slumping to the ground. David was on top of him.

"I'm going to beat the shit out of you."

Charlie was on his feet again. "You *took* her." He punched David's right arm. "You *took* her!"

They grappled. David plowed his forehead into Charlie's chest, beating furiously on his stomach.

"*You* stole her from *me*!" he shouted. "She's not yours!"

"She's not yours!"

They were on the ground, writhing between the cars. Charlie had never felt so connected to his body. Every punch David landed was exquisite. Every blow he delivered was joy. He felt himself release, everything inside him flowing out like the blood that dripped from his nose, pattering onto the sidewalk, onto the front of David's shirt, mixing with the blood from David's lip.

"Screw you! Screw you!" David screamed.

Charlie screamed back a litany of gibberish. David's palm pressed against Charlie's forehead. His knee landed hard in Charlie's stomach. Charlie shoved his elbow into David's shoulder and punched him in the side. David shoved back so hard, Charlie's own fist hit him in the face. He couldn't tell where David ended and he began.

Charlie felt someone pull hard on his jacket. He was jerked back and landed on his butt. A uniformed officer stood over him.

"What the hell's going on here?"

Another cop held back David, who clawed at Charlie's pant leg. David's mouth was contorted into a strange grimace, and Charlie saw tears rolling down his cheeks.

"Stop it! Stop it!" the other cop shouted. "Jesus, boy. Calm down."

Charlie felt his rage drain away. His heart pounded, he was breathing hard, but he felt calm. It was over.

He rubbed his palms on his jeans. They were crusted with grit. His shirt was a bloody purple.

One officer put a heavy hand on Charlie's shoulder — not a friendly gesture.

"What the hell do you think you're doing? You can't just beat the hell out of each other in the middle of a parking lot. You want to do that in the school yard, fine. Then it's your principal's problem. Here, it's mine."

The other officer released David, who'd stopped struggling. He stared at the ground, snorted, and spat blood.

"You wanna book 'em?"

The first cop rubbed his chin, then shook his head. "Naw."

The second cop nodded.

"But if I have to break you two up again, I'll throw you both in the cruiser, got it?"

Charlie nodded.

The cop released his shoulder and marched back to the barricade. His partner followed. "Twenty bucks says it's over a girl."

David and Charlie sat on the curb and watched the Sakora guys load the last of May's stolen equipment into the van. They stayed until the street was empty and the green neon clock above the bank flashed 1:00. David put his head in his hands.

"What did they tell you?" Charlie asked

David took a breath. "That they could bring her back. And also make her forget."

"Forget that you kicked her out?"

"Yeah."

"She would have come back to you," Charlie said. "She would have forgiven you. At first, anyway."

David spat onto the curb. "I don't think they're going to bring her back."

"No," Charlie said. "Your lip still bleeding?"

"A little." He stood up.

"Where are you going?"

"Home."

Charlie biked home. Pedaling took a conscious effort. Thaddeus didn't ask him where he'd been, and in the morning, when he left for school, Thaddeus patted him on the back and gave him a reassuring smile.

A door opened, Charlie wanted to tell him, and then it closed again, too fast for him to really see what was on the other side.

David wasn't in school that day, nor the day after. When he returned, he nodded to Charlie in the hall, the barest sign of recognition. Charlie didn't know that first day, but the nod would become a kind of tradition. Over the next few weeks, every morning when Charlie came to homeroom, David would nod, and Charlie would give a half-articulated "Hey." This was the one ripple in the pond of their everyday existence, the otherwise unchanging glassy surface of their lives. David was still David; Charlie was still Charlie. Same as always.

At semester's end, Charlie went to see the play. Rebecca, who'd decided to rejoin, was brilliant, even though she was only in two scenes. (Willow Watts's Eliza Doolittle was atrocious.) The program read *In Loving Memory of Nora*

Vogel. Charlie waited for Rebecca at the stage door with a bouquet of lavender and peonies, and they walked around to the front of Saint Seb's, where a group of pigeons, displaced by cars parked on the grass, roosted on the statue's spokes, along with that old necktie, still ensnared. Grinning, Charlie ran toward them, squawking and flapping his arms. The startled birds burst up in a gray plume. Rebecca's laughter thundered as he swung back for another pass. The birds were already settling back, except for one red-tipped flutter that spiraled up in a gust of wind.

Then one night Charlie was out riding when he saw flashing lights across the lake. He rode down the hill toward a pair of police cruisers. David's Cadillac had run off the road and was nearly into the lake. The front end was half-submerged. The guardrail was broken, and a pair of tracks drew straight muddy lines from the road to the bank. Otherwise there didn't seem to be much damage. David sat on the back bumper of the ambulance, a blanket wrapped around his shoulders, looking pale but unharmed. The car was only partway submerged; David must have regained control enough to brake before driving all the way into the water. But from Charlie's vantage point it looked like the lake stopped the car, as if the water wasn't water but an impermeable barrier the luxury automobile didn't have the strength to shatter.

16. Over and Over

There was water in the Caddy's engine, and the onboard computer was permanently fried. David suffered worse from his parents.

"Were you drinking?"

"He's high right now! Look at his eyes!"

"You *terrified* us."

"Do you see what you're doing to your mother?"

David stared at the ground.

"You're grounded," said Mr. Sun. Then, into his headset, "No, not you, Larry. Talking to the kid."

The grounding itself wasn't so bad — only a week. David guessed they felt guilty. Sakora had been their bad idea, after all. It was their fault he was depressed. Or so he let them think. And he was depressed. He didn't need Dr. Roger to tell him that.

He walked at night, something he'd never done before. On foot it was difficult to find his way. He'd memorized the back roads from the vantage point of a bucket seat, and on his quieter, slower rambles he frequently got lost. He recognized nothing.

What had happened? He'd been driving too fast — a simple idea that didn't need explanation. But he kept returning to that question over and over again. *What happened?* He liked to drive fast, and this time he'd gone too fast. It didn't *mean* anything. So his foot slipped, or he was distracted. It was definitely an accident, absolutely. So why should it matter so much to him? The point was the result — his car was totaled, and he was walking around in the woods like a hobo.

At night it was so black he had trouble seeing his hand in front of his face. It got his mind going, thinking crazy thoughts. What if he was changing? What if he was becoming a wolf-man or some slimy, scaly thing with suckers on his fingers? In the dark he couldn't tell. On some nights he scared himself so bad he'd rush home, just to turn on the lights. And somehow, when he saw himself in the hall mirror, and saw that he hadn't changed, he felt almost disappointed.

One night, two weeks after the crash, he began to wonder if he was dead. He knew he wasn't really dead — he'd just been on the phone with Willow, and ghosts didn't text-message. But just . . . what if? What if his spirit was wandering around the woods, only thinking it was alive? David didn't believe in heaven or hell, but it made sense that a ghost would hang around the place where he died, as if he were trying to climb back inside the world, though the door had shut behind him.

David found himself by the lake. The moon reflected in the black, near-frozen surface. And then David saw what looked like a real ghost in the water. Something white glided toward the shore. David froze, his mind shouting at his legs to run. And then the ghost broke the surface, and he saw it was Charlie Nuvola, out for a midnight swim in sub-zero weather.

"What are you doing?"

Charlie looked up. Not surprised, just curious. Instead of answering, he sloshed onto the bank. There was a duffel bag waiting for him. He pulled out a towel and three pairs of sweats. There was steam rising off his moony skin. He pulled the sweats on, and only then did he seem cold, his teeth chattering.

"Aren't you freezing?"

"My dad and I used to do the polar-bear plunge at Olive Lake when I was a kid," he said. He put on a fur-lined coat and laced up a pair of heavy-duty hiking boots. "This isn't even fully frozen." Charlie paused to stare out at the water. "It's so deep. Deeper than a regular lake, you know. Because it's a reservoir."

"That's what they say."

David wanted to get away from him. It was creepy—finding Charlie of all people, swimming in the middle of the night in December.

"It's deeper at this end," he said. "When they dynamited the rock, they ended up going deeper over here. It's kind of like a big swimming pool, with a deep end and a shallow end. I'm surprised you don't see more people swimming in it."

"It's illegal to swim in it," David said.

Charlie shrugged. "Lots of things are illegal."

David zipped his jacket to his chin and stuffed his hands in his pockets. They were done talking. But he lingered a moment by the shore.

"Do you think she's still . . . ?" David searched for the word, but he already knew it. "Do you think she's still alive?"

Charlie nodded. "I don't think," he said without hesitation. "I *know* she is. In fact, I . . ." But he stopped himself, watching David.

David opened his mouth to reply. A car horn cut him off. Headlights swept the trees and the gravel rustled as a busted Cadillac pulled off Cliff Road. Charlie gathered his things and jogged toward the passenger door.

"That's my ride." He turned back to David. "Do you want a lift?"

David said nothing. Charlie waited another beat, then climbed inside. The driver was a dark-haired girl David knew from somewhere. The car reversed and pulled onto the road. David watched the brake lights as they came to the intersection of Cliff and Horizon, and then broke away from the lake's circle, down Route 28A, bathing the night in crimson before disappearing from view.

It was a long, slow, cold walk home.

When he got in, he called Willow. They talked a lot lately. Clay and Artie had razzed him about it, said he was on the rebound. But David could tell it didn't bother them too much. If anything, they seemed relieved he'd moved on. He was amazed how he and Willow could pick up where they'd left off, like a sequel to a movie, where they use all the same jokes.

That night they v-chatted for hours. David liked her face on his monitor, her thin red lips and golden hair. He kept her vid-window open in the center on Mon2. As they talked, Mon3 flashed away, pages on dating advice, dinner reservations for two, even blond hair dye. Mon1 took its cue and showed famous blondes like Marilyn — Mon2 popped up black-and-white vids from Retro_Flix.com. Mon3 scrolled old-time movie quotes, then the post from Starry-EyedStranger42 flitted by: *If I had done this a long time ago, it would have saved a lot of pain.* — *Peg Entwistle.*

The pages cycled as David and Willow joked, feeding on each other, around and around, over and over, everything associated. With all the lights on and the monitors going and his music on the speakers and Willow's bright smile, David felt better, and forgot about everything unconnected.

ACKNOWLEDGMENTS

My deepest gratitude to my agent and mentor, Scott Treimel, for all he has done for this book and its author. A very special thanks to Deborah Noyes Wayshak, my editor, who believed in this story and helped make it shine. Many thanks, and much, much love to Sarah Elmaleh, my first reader and best friend. Thanks to Kit Reed and David Vilandre, who taught me so much about writing. Thank you to all my wonderful and supportive friends. Thanks to all the people who inspired characters, glances, images, and sensations in this book. And thank you to all the authors, living and dead, who have been my dearest companions.

John M. Cusick is from a small town in Massachusetts and is a 2007 graduate of Wesleyan University. About *Girl Parts,* he says, "It is easy to feel lonely, despite the immediacy of technological connection. This is a story about human connections, how they catch us by surprise and challenge who we are." A literary agent of books for children and teens, John M. Cusick lives in Brooklyn.